"A lyrical tale of a unique culture. I loved it."
—Patricia C. Wrede, author of
THE SEVEN TOWERS

"Jane Yolen's CARDS OF GRIEF is one of the
most moving and powerful books I have ever
read. Each individual story is a complete,
flawless gem, and the book in its entirety is
breathtaking. She is frighteningly good."
—Steven Brust, author of
YENDI

"CARDS OF GRIEF is a seamless blend of the
tensions of good science fiction and the rhythms
of myth. . . . A graceful and powerful work
from the Queen Mother of story telling."
—Diane Duane, author of
THE DOOR INTO FIRE

Other fantasy titles available from
Ace Science Fiction and Fantasy

The Face in the Frost, *John Bellairs*
Ariel: A Book of the Change, *Steven R. Boyett*
The Borribles, *Michael de Larrabeiti*
The Broken Citadel, *Joyce Ballou Gregorian*
Songs From the Drowned Lands, *Eileen Kernaghan*
Annals of Klepsis, *R. A. Lafferty*
Swords and Deviltry, *Fritz Leiber*
Khi to Freedom, *Ardath Mayhar*
The Door in the Hedge, *Robin McKinley*
Jirel of Joiry, *C. L. Moore*
Witch World, *Andre Norton*
The Anubis Gates, *Tim Powers*
Tomoe Gozen, *Jessica Amanda Salmonson*
The Warlock Unlocked, *Christopher Stasheff*
Bard, *Keith Taylor*
The Devil in a Forest, *Gene Wolfe*
The Seven Towers, *Patricia C. Wrede*
Changeling, *Roger Zelazny*

and much more!

CARDS OF GRIEF

Jane Yolen

ACE FANTASY BOOKS
NEW YORK

CARDS OF GRIEF

An Ace Fantasy Book/published by arrangement with the author

PRINTING HISTORY
Ace Original/December 1984

ISBN: 0-441-09166-0

Ace Fantasy Books are published by
The Berkley Publishing Group,
200 Madison Avenue, New York, New York 10016.
PRINTED IN THE UNITED STATES OF AMERICA

For Georgia and Milton
and all the cloud-filled skies

ARCHIVIST'S REPORT

Here are the preliminary tapes and reports on our one-hundred-year study of Henderson's IV, known in the common tongue as L'Lal'lor, the Planet of the Grievers.

As with all one-hundred-year studies, the first fifty are done SS (Surreptitious Surveillance), including planet mapping, flora and fauna studies, geologic probes, infrared night photography. Whenever there is a viable intelligence within the native populations, we also implant long-lived voice-activated recorders randomly which aid in the study of language and culture.

The second fifty years consist of open visits by anthropologists, linguists, historians, but always AD (Arm's Distance). We are observers only. We try not to influence the history of a planet or contaminate a living culture, but occasionally—as in the contact with the inhabitants of Henderson's IV—mistakes are made.

In this particular study, it is essential to keep in mind that life aboard the space lab accounts for one year per ten on planetfall due to the Hulanlocke Rotational Device, so that this one-hundred-year study took ten years subjective or labtime.

These preliminary tapes are not arranged chronologically but in a manner that will allow the listener to understand the nature of the culture contamination.

Planetfall: Henderson's IV is a water planet with only one major continental land mass.

Species contacted: High intelligence life forms; humanoid; two distinct morphs; two distinct sexes.

Society: Clan format; six great endomorphic families representing general labor groups ruled by seventh which is ectomorphic and near barren; matriarchal descent pattern; blocked technology at approximately Bronze; high artistic levels.

Biology, Geology: Reports to come.

Histo-Archeologist's Synoptic: There is strong geologic evidence of a catastrophic flood having covered the face of the planet within the last millennium, said evidence supported by oral tradition of the master singers and poets. Said flood left only the highest mountains untouched. (See work entitled *Shells in Strata*, sub. 4 Geologist's Report.) Those mountaintops are honeycombed with enormous caves that lead into unlit fuliginous-sided caverns filled with fossilized tree residue, evidence of hearthfires. The surrounding valleys retain humanoid bones in a scattered pattern suggesting exposure rather than burial as the prime manner of disposing of the dead. Modern L'Lal'lorians, with their cat's eyes and fine night sight, with their culture emphasis on caves as a place of dying but not of burial, are a logical consequence both physically and culturally of a cave-dwelling past.

The matriarchal system is an outgrowth of the small live-birth ratio and early infant death syndrome, i.e., females, the bearers, are highly valued. Since the flood at least, only a small section of land has been salvaged from—or given up by—the sea; the population has grown only enough to comfortably fill the island continent. The people are in-bred, the resultant culture homogenous. The only thing that keeps the breed as hardy as it is is the custom of polyandry and of sending the nearly sterile male Royals on a long coming-of-age journey, ostensibly for gaining cultural perspective. In fact it encourages a mixing of the small gene pool and the occasional resultant ectomorphs are nearly always the most talented and intelligent of their groups, taking on leadership roles easily.

Anthropologist's Synoptic: This grief-centered culture is not to be confused with the death-centered societies such as those found on Atropos or Maytec or our own early Egyptian. Rather the L'Lal'lorians revere life and do not fear death, though they live life in a kind of gray haze, without laughter or passion. Still, there is no war nor any racial memory of large conflicts, no infanticide, little murder except where ordered by the ruler, no theft. There is, however, a form of suicide widely practiced by the older L'Lal'lorians as an escape from any wasting terminal illnesses. It is ritualized, painless, and quick. Confession before such a death is important and the choice of the confessor not often left to chance.

The grieving, which is as much art as religion, is the L'Lal'lorian way of remembering, an artistic bid for continuity, for they believe in no substantial afterlife and there is no evidence whatsoever of a belief in reincarnation. Unlike our own seventeenth-century poet Thomas Carew who wrote, "Grief is a puddle and reflects not cleare," grieving for the L'Lal'lorians is a clear reflection of their societal needs and a recording of their prehistory in caves. And while at first glance it may seem no more than a parody of Earth customs such as tomb decoration (N.B. Falkowitz's essay on Italian grave decor, *The Journal of the Folklore Society*, 1997:2) or a trade show (N.B. Morrissey-White "A Study in the Ad Biz," Harvard Press Monographic Series 2037), this planet is an untouched humanoid society and we have been First Contact. The customs are their own.

To observe, to study, to learn: those are the words of the Anthropologist's Guild.

Note****Note****Note**** Culture Contact Contamination by Anthropologist First Class Aaron Spenser, B.S., M.S., Ph.D., Star Certificate 9876433680K. Court Martial records herewith. Sentence five years space lab, equal to fifty years on-planet. In his favor, Anthropologist First Class Spenser's work on the culture of Henderson's IV has been invaluable and while he has since GN (gone native), it is included in the Synoptic and elsewhere.

Enclosed prelim tapes and studies

Tape 1:

THE SEVEN GRIEVERS, PART I

Place: *Queen's Hall of Grief, Room of Instruction*

Time: *Queen's Time 23, Thirteenth Matriarchy; labtime 2132.5+ A.D.*

Speaker: *Queen's Own Griever to the apprentices, including Lina-Lania*

Permission: *No permission, preset, voice-activated*

This is the song of the Seven Grievers, the seven great families of L'Lal'lor, from the days and nights of the sky's grieving to the very moment of my tongue's speaking. I have held these dolorous chants in my mind and in my heart against the time when, as the Queen's Own Griever, I may have to wail for the wasting of our land once again.

The first time our land died it was in water; but of water we may speak only at birth when water gushes forth unbidden from the cave of the womb, or at grieving when the waters flow at our bidding from our sorrowing eyes.

The next time the land dies, say the prophesies, will be when we forget to grieve.

It is written in the sky; it is written in the rocks; it is written in the sea; it is written on our hearts. But nowhere is it to be written down in any scripting of our own devising, for such is forbidden lest we then forget how to read it. To hold in the mouth is to remember; to set down is to forget. This sacred knowledge, therefore, must be passed Griever to

1

Griever, Master to Master, mouth to ear, down through all time.

Hear then, listen well. My word is firm, firmer than sleep or the Cup that carries it, firmer than the strength of heroes. My voice makes the telling true. To listen, to remember, is to know.

Before the weeping of the sky, the land was soft and plentiful and there was no grief. Light bathed the land always and there was no division between the day and the night, between the bright and the dark. So there was no cold, no hunger, no hurt, and no dying. The world was called L'Lal'ladia, the Place of Blessing and Rejoicing.

But the People grew tired of such beauty and constant light. They turned to the dark of the caves and to games of chance. They pricked blood from their own arms to count the flow. And so the very skies began to weep blood. For one hundred times one hundred days water fell from the cloudless sky, first red and then clear, until the bowl of the world was filled with it. And all but two who dwelled in L'Lal'ladia and were called the People were drowned. Those two were a man and a woman, and he past the years of seeding. Even the light itself was put out, like a candle between wet fingers, leaving but a gray sooty smudge in the sky.

Then there crept from the caves in the highest mountains a second people called Night-Seers who lit watchfires in the day that lifted smoke into the now darkening sky. They sang their heavy songs and they called to the blackness and there was no rejoicing in their hearts. And for one hundred times one hundred nights the world turned black and was lit only by the softly falling stars.

The one arose from the Night-Seers and said, "Let us cast down great stones into the water that we may frighten it back from the land."

So one by one they rolled down great stones until the water was thrust back, leaving a land that was black as night and rich with the meat of fish and covered with strange bones.

And the smell of that land was strong and hunger called down a few of the Night-Seers onto the plains where they went about, back and forth, through the mud and left the marks of their feet and the prints of their hands as if carved deep into stone. And these few took up their lives on the muddy flats.

And a few of the Night-Seers were called on farther by the salt smell of the sea and followed the receding water to the place where sea and land met and wrestled for the ruling. Here the few Night-Seers stopped and cast their nets far into the water and pulled in their livings from the sea.

But the rest of the Night-Seers still hid in the shadows of the mountains, for they swore they knew the hilly wastes best and there they lived forever.

So the first of the Seven Grievers were these:

> **Lands**, who live on the plains,
> stockmen and farmers, harrowers and
> pigkeepers, tillers of soil and grinders
> of grain.

> **Waters**, who dwell by the sea and
> harvest with cunningly wrought nets
> the little finny creatures that swim
> close to shore.

Rocks, who live in the shadow of the mountains and carve out the face of the stone, crafting jewels and gems, and building blocks.

But from the time of the hundred times a hundred days and the hundred times a hundred nights, and in memory of the time the sky itself wept first blood and then rain, grieving has been the way of remembering and the one great art of our world. And the world is no longer called L'Lal'ladia, the Place of Blessing and Rejoicing, but is called L'Lal'loria, the Place of the Grievers.

Selah.

Tape 2:

IN THE HALL
OF GRIEF

Place: Cave #27

Time: King's Time 1, First Patriarchy; labtime
2137.5 + A.D.

Speaker: Lina-Lania, known as the Gray
Wanderer, to her apprentice Grenna

Permission: None, preset, voice-activated

I was thirteen summers, the last turning of childhood, when Great-grandmother became ill. She was
exiled upstairs to the windowless room under the
thatch to practice lying in darkness. So it is with the
very old whose lives are spent in dusk, just as new-
borns must learn to live in the dawn.

It was not Great-grandmother's illness that made
me eligible to enter the Hall of Grief but my own
signs of adulthood: the small breasts just beginning
to bud, the fine curlings of hair in the cave places
of my body, the rush of fresh blood from the un-
tested nest of my womb.

I was ready. Had I not spent many childhood
hours playing at the Hall game? Alone or with my
brothers I had built our own Halls of willow branch
and mallo snappings. We had set the tables, made
signs, drawn pictures. Always, always my table was
best, though I was not the oldest of us all. My table
had more than just an innocent beauty, decked in
ribbons and bordered by wildflowers: red trillis for
life, blue-black mourning berries for death, and the
twining of green boughs for the passage between.

No, my table had a character that was both mine and the grieven one's. It had substance and imagination and daring, even from the time I was quite young. Everyone remarked on it. The other children sensed it and a few resented it. But the elders who came and watched us at our play, they knew for sure. I heard one say, "She has a gift for grief, that one. Mark her well." As if my height and the angularity of my body had not marked me already.

But even before that I had known. As a child I had started crafting my own grief poems, childishly lisping them to my dolls. The first poems aped the dirges and threnodies I had been taught, but always with a little twist of my own. One in particular I remember, for my mother shared it with the elders as a sign of my gift. My grandmother argued against that poem and for another, but this quarrel my mother won. The poem began:

> I sail out on my dark ship
> Toward the unmarked shore
> With only the grievings
> Of my family to guide me.
> The ship breasts the waves . . .

The dark ship, the unmarked shore—they were but copies of the usual metaphors of grief. But the wording of the fifth line, the *penta*—which foreshadowed the central image, that of a carved figurehead of a nude woman, something of which I should have had no knowledge, for we were a people of the Middle Lands, tillers of soil and grinders of grain—that fifth line convinced them. I, the daughter of a miller, gangly and stalk-legged, I was a prodigy. I basked in their praises for weeks and tried to repeat my success, but that time I could not. My subsequent poems were banal; they showed no promise at all. It was years before I realized that, truly, I grieved best when trying for no effect at all, though the critics and the public and the silly men at court did not always know the difference. But the craftswoman knows.

And then the day came when I was old enough to enter the Hall of Grief. I rose early and spent many minutes in front of the glass, the only one in our house not then covered with the gray mourning cloth. I drew dark circles under my eyes and deep shades on my lids as befitted a griever. Of course I overdid it. What new griever does not? I had yet to learn that true grief makes its own hollows in the face, a better sculptor of the body's contours than all our paints and pens. Artifice should only heighten. But I was young, as I have said, and even Great-grandmother in her dusky room was not enough to teach me then.

That first day I tried something daring. Even that first day my gift for invention showed. I painted my nails the color of my eyelids and, on the left hand, on the thumb, I took a penknife and scraped the paint on the thumbnail into a cross to signify the bisecting of life and death.

Yes, I see you understand. It was the beginning of the carvings I would later do on all my nails, the carvings that would become such a passion among young grievers at court and be given my name. I never do it myself anymore. It seemed such a little thing, then: some extra paint, an extra dab of darkness onto light. An instinctual gesture that others took—mistook—for genius. That is, after all, what genius is: a label for instinct,

I plaited my long hair with trillis and mourning berry, too. And that was much less successful. As I recall, the trillis died before half a day was over and the berries left my braids sticky with juice. Yet at the moment of leavetaking, when I went upstairs to give Great-grandmother the respect I owed her, I felt the proper griever.

She turned in her bed, the one with the carvings of wreaths on the posters, the one in which all the women of our house have died. The air in the room was close and still. Even I had trouble breathing. Then Great-grandmother looked at me with her luminous half-dead eyes, the signs of pain beginning to stretch her mouth wide. She was ill with something that gnawed inside her.

"You will make them remember me?" she asked.

Knowing my mother and grandmother must have already made the same promise before they left, I nevertheless replied, "Great-grandmother, I will."

"May your lines of grieving be long," she said.

"May your time of dying be short," I answered, and the ritual was complete.

I left at once, not even checking to see if the Cup on the table by the bed was filled. I was far more interested in the Hall of Grief and my part in it than in my Great-grandmother's actual time of death, when the breath leaps from the wide mouth in an upward sigh. That is, after all, a private moment and grieving is a public act. At thirteen I longed to show my grief in public and win the applause and my Great-grandmother's immortality. I know now that all our mourning, all our grieving, all the outward signs of our rituals are nothing compared to that one quick moment of release. Do I startle you with my heresy? Ah, child, heresy is the prerogative of old age.

I did not look back at the dark room, but ran down the stairs and into the welcoming light. My mother and her mother had already gone to the Hall. I marched there to the slow metronome of the funerary drums, which cousins of my cousins were always trained to play, but my heart skipped before.

The Hall was even larger than I had dreamed. Great massive pillars with fluted columns and carved capitols held up the roof. I had seen the building from afar—for who had not; it dominated our small town square. But I had never been allowed close enough to really distinguish the carvings. They were appropriate to a Hall, weeping women with their long hair caught up in fanciful waterfalls. You laugh. Only in the countryside could such banal motifs still be seen. It was a very minor Hall to be sure, but to my eyes then it was magnificent, each marble weeper a monument to grief. I drank it all in, eager to be part.

I told the guard at the gate my name and clan and he sent a runner in. My mother appeared shortly and spoke in quiet undertones to the gatekeeper, assuring him that it was my time. He let me in with a brief smile that slit open between the parenthesis of his mustache.

We walked up stairs that were hollowed by years of marchers and entered the Hall. Inside, the clans had already set up their tables and Mother threaded her way through the chaos to our usual stand with an ease born of long experience. Under the banner proclaiming our colors and the sign of the millstone was a kidney-shaped table. It was littered with the memoria of our dying ones. We had had three diers

that year, counting Great-grandmother now in our
attic. I can still recite the birth lines of the other
two: Cassa-Cania, of Chriss-Cania, of Cassua-
Cania, of Camma-Cania was the one. Peri-Pania, of
Perri-Pania, of Persa-Pania, of Parsis-Pania was the
other. And of course, in my own direct line I can
still go back the twenty-one requisite names. We
had no gap in that line, the Lania, of which I am
still, though it sometimes makes me laugh at myself,
inordinately proud. I am really the last of the Lania.
No one will grieve for me properly, no sister of the
family, no blood child, and sometimes it troubles
me that this is so, my own tiny sisters having gone
before me when I was too young to grieve for them
and my brothers unable to carry on the line.

The daughters of Cassa-Cania and Peri-Pania
were already there, having no attic grieven of their
own and no new grievers to prepare for their first
Hall. They, poor ones, had born only boys. And of
course my own little sisters had gone in one of the
winter sicknesses, their tiny mouths stretched wide
in the smile of death, their eyelids closed under the
carved funerary gems. Though I had not officially
grieved for them, I had certainly practiced grief in
my games with the boys.

Our table was piled high with pictographs of their
dyings, for of course that was before the strangers
had come down from the sky with their strange
cam'ras that captured life impressions on a small
page. And since Cassa-Cania's daughters were
known for their fine hand, there were many ornately
lettered lamentation plaques on the table. But for
all its wealth of memoria, the table appeared disordered to me and that disturbed me greatly.

I spoke in an undertone to my mother. "May I be allowed to arrange Great-grandmother's part?"

At first she shook her head and her dark graying hair fell loose of its crown, cascading down over her shoulders like the weeping women of the column. But it was simply that she did not understand my distress at the disorder, taking my request as a display of adolescent eagerness. However, I was still thought to be too young to do more than watch and listen—and learn. I had yet to be apprenticed to a griever, to one of the older cousins. I had, for all my reputed genius, only a meager background, the pretendings of a child with children (and brothers at that). I knew no history, could recite none of the prime tales, and could only mouth a smattering of the lesser songs and stories of the People. So I was sent away while the older women worked; I was sent off to look at the other tables in the Hall, to discover for myself the many stages and presentations of Grief.

Alas, the other tables were as disordered as our own, for as I have said, we were only a very Minor Hall and the grievers there were unsophisticated in their arrangements. One or two had a rough feeling I have since tried to replicate in my own work. Touching the old country grief has, I think, given me my greatest successes.

To think of it, walking in a Hall before the days of the strangers from the sky, walking in it for the very first time. The sound of the mourners lining up in the galleries, waiting for the doors to open. Some of them actually wailed their distress, though in the Major Halls that rarely happens anymore, except on great occasions of state—an exiled princess, the assassination of a prince, a fallen Queen. Most of the time the older princes gossip rather than weep, and the younger ones are too ready to make an impression on the Queen.

But that Minor Hall was not a place of Queens or princes. Grief actually walked there. I could feel it start in my belly and creep up into my throat. Only that I was inside and not beyond the doors kept me from wailing, too, for inside the grievers moved silently, setting up the stalls. I remember one old woman lovingly polishing a hoe, the symbol of the farmer her dying granduncle had been. She stood under the sign of a grainfield and she rocked back and forth beneath it as if the wind that tossed the grain on her sign tossed her as well. There is another I remember: a woman with ten black ribbons in her hair, placing a harp with a broken string beside a lamentation plaque that read: *One last song, one final touch.* I have always liked the simplicity of that line, though the broken string was a bit overdone.

Then the doors were flung open and the mourners came in. In the first crush I lost sight of our own table and was pushed up against the wall. If I had been smaller, I might have panicked, but the one great gift of body that I had was height. I was at least as tall at thirteen as an adult, as tall as the smallest of the princes even then.

Soon the crowds sorted themselves and I could see how the lines made a kind of pattern. There were long lines by the tables that gave away garlands and crying cloths, though the longest by far was in front of the harper's stall where a live singer—a princeling on his mission year—recalled in song all that had been great in the harper's life. He used the old songs, of course, and set the facts in the open measures of the songs with such facility and with such a good sense of rhythm that it was never apparent what was old and what was interpolated.

I learned two things that day, before ever apprenticing: to please the crowd and draw a line is easy, but to keep the lines coming back again and again is not. Once the garlands were gone and the cloths given away, once the singer stopped for a draught of wine, the line of mourners broke apart and formed again elsewhere. And none of the mourners remembered the grieven one's name for longer than that day, though some remembered the names of the grievers. There is no immortality in that.

By noon I had toured the entire Hall, carrying with me a wilted garland and three cloths embroidered with names of grieven ones whose deeds I no longer recalled. And I came back again to the place I had begun, the stall of my own clan under the millstone, piled high with disordered memoria.

"Let me take a turn while you eat. It will be a slow time, now, while the funeral meats are set out," I told my aunts and my mother, my grandmother having gone home to tend to mill business and to prepare her mother's last meal. They thought I could do no harm then, when most mourners were off eating or doing their home chores. It was neither planting nor harvesting time, so there would be an afternoon grieving in the Hall, but that would not be for a while. They left me at the table.

I busied myself at once, rearranging the overwrought items in a new way so that the whole picture was one of restraint. And then I sat down and composed a threnody, the first of the ones recognizable in my so-called Gray Wanderer period, because for the first time the figure of the cloaked soul-traveler appeared. The words seemed to tumble into

d, the stanzas and chorus forming as if on a
. in fact the poem wrote itself, and quickly. In
later years I was to force myself to slow down, for
I have always had a facility that, at times, betrays
me.

You know the poem, of course: "The lines of her
worn and gray cloak . . ." You are nodding, child.
Does it seem strange to you that someone real wrote
a song that you have known all your life? Well, I
wrote it as if in a fever that day. It all seemed to fit.
I never thought that I would be called the Gray Wanderer myself—I, who have never wandered very far
and whose life has never seemed exceptionally gray.
Of course the scholars insist that "the lines of her
worn and gray cloak" refer to the lines of mourning.
I did not mean that, just that the cloak fell from her
shoulders in comfortable, familiar folds. That is how
I saw the Gray Wanderer that day in the eye of my
mind. Perhaps it was my great-grandmother I was
seeing, bent over a bit but still strong despite the
thing that ate away at her. But never mind. Scholars
seem to know more about such things than we grievers do.

You are smiling. You have heard me say all this
before. Do I, in my age and illness, repeat myself
endlessly? Well, what else is there to do, lying here
in the darkness, but retrace the steps of light? Here
I throw no shadows and that is how it should be.
But once my shadow—the shadow of the Gray
Wanderer—covered the entire land. I guess there
is a certain pride in that, and a certain immortality.

I remember I had just finished the threnody in
my head and was tracing out the words onto a tablet.
It was slow going. I had not the grace of my aunts'
hands and each letter had to be painstakingly drawn.

You have such hand's grace, child, and that is one
of the reasons—though not the only one—why I
kept you past your training. No, do not blush. You
know it is true. Do not confuse humility with self-
denial. You have an old hand grafted onto a young
arm. Not for you are the easy strangers' ways, the
machines from their great ships that multiply letters.
Hold on to the best of the old ways, child. Pass them
on.

Yes, I drew the words slowly and my hand fal-
tered on a phrase. Oh, the phrase was fine, but the
lettering was traitor to its truth. I was casting around
for a scraper when I realized that someone was
standing over me. I looked up and it was a youth
just past that blush of boyhood, when the skin still
had a lambent glow yet is covered with soft down
that has not yet coarsened into a beard. It was the
singer, the princeling. Before, I had concentrated
on his singing, which had been very lovely. Close
by, I was overcome by his beauty. He was tall, of
course, and his bones more finely drawn than any
of our Lands men. And he had a quick though in-
frequent smile, not the slow vanishing slits of mouth
and teeth that my brothers and their friends used.

"I would have liked them," he said in his low,
ripe voice. He nodded at the memoria to my great-
grandmother and great-great-aunts.

It is the ritual opening, to be sure, the mildest
approach to an unknown grieven one. But somehow
I sensed it was sincerely meant. And though I answered with the words that have been spoken already a thousand thousand times by grievers, he
knew my own sincerity in them.

"They would have grown by your friendship."

I scraped the linen free of the mistake and finished the threnody while he watched. I blushed under his scrutiny. My face was always a slate on which my emotions were writ too large, and I have carefully schooled myself against such displays. I pulled the linen free of its stretcher. The linen curled up at the edges just a bit, which was what I had hoped. It meant a reader had to flatten it by hand and in that way actually participate in the reading.

He took the time to read it, not once but several times. And then he read it aloud. His voice, already changed, had been trained since birth. He was to be a member of the Queen's Consort and she had only the best. In his mouth the words I had written took on an even more palpable sense of grief. A fine singer can make a song, you know.

Soon we were surrounded by the other table watchers. He knew how to project his voice, he was a prince after all, and the others caught phrases that beckoned them, drew them in.

And that was how my mother and my great-aunts found us when they returned, with a long line of mourners standing under the millstone sign. All the other stalls were empty, even of watchers. The mourners were saying with him, as he repeated the threnody yet one more time, the chorus that is now so famous:

> Weep for the night that is coming,
> Weep for the day that is past.

Yes, it is simple. Every child knows it now, in the time of the strangers. But I wrote it that day when the strangers were not even a dream, and I wove my great-grandmother's name into the body of the poem that she would not be forgotten. Her lines were long indeed. I was glad to have done it that day, for she was dead when we returned home and already my brothers had set out her husk on the pyre and pylons for the birds of prey.

The next seven days, as true grievers, we mourned upon the stage of the Hall for our grieven one's passage to the world of everlasting Light. How my great-grandmother must have smiled at her lines of mourning. Such long, loyal lines. My mother said there had never been such lines in our Minor Hall except when the singer Verina died who had been born in the town next but one to ours and whose relatives numbered in the hundreds in the countryside. My grandmother disagreed, mentioning a painter whose name I had never heard of and whose lines, she claimed, had been longer. But then my mother and grandmother always found things to disagree about. They agreed, though, that the longest lines had been for the last Queen, though that had been well before my mother's time and when my grandmother had been but a girl.

I wrote three more Gray Wanderer threnodies and one thirty-two-verse dirge which the harper prince set to a modal tune. The Hall throbbed with it for days, though one can hear it only occasionally now. It takes too long in the singing, and the strangers brought with them a taste for short songs. But Great-grandmother has not been forgotten and I still have pride in that, for I made it so.

After the seven days, it was incumbent upon my mother to find me a Master Griever from our clan, though, by tradition, there should have been a year between my first entrance into a Hall and any formal apprenticeship. But the elders had come to her as soon as the Seven was over. They even spoke in front of me, which was unheard-of at that time.

"She must be trained now, while the grace of tongue is still with her," said one. She was a hen-keeper by trade who had lost her own voice young and still mourned it.

My mother agreed.

By habit, my grandmother disagreed. "There is no one here worthy of our Linni," she argued.

"Do you not have some long connection on the coast?" asked another Elder. She was unfamiliar to me, though the white streak in her hair proclaimed her of Nadia's line.

"We do not have the means," my mother began.

"We will borrow if needs be," my grandmother said. As she was now head of the Lania, I knew it would be so.

They argued it out over and over as we walked home. I felt the injustice of my mother's stand, though in my heart I did not want to impoverish them for my poetry's sake. They ignored me and no one asked me what I wished. And what did I wish? For some magic to descend upon us all and make us wealthy or take me away somewhere, so that I could do nothing but make my poems in peace.

That very day there came a knock on the door. Ah, I see you are ahead of me. Have I told this before? It was the singer, B'oremos, the prince from the Hall. He had left after the first day, gone—I had assumed—to finish his young man's pilgrimage from Hall to Hall. I had hoped that he would stay awhile but I had only my words to hold him. In those early days, knowing the pull of the plump and lovely Lands girls on the princes, I did not value my own talents enough. I knew he would be there only a short while at best. I did not want to be the only girl in our village who had been slighted by a prince. Of course he had already paid me a great deal of attention, but that was part of his training, singing for different mourners, setting their threnodies to tunes. I had hoped he might stay over with us and instead he had left precipitously. But he had not gone on along his route, though, forgetting me for some saucy pigkeeper's daughter. Instead he had doubled back and told the Queen herself what had happened in our Hall. It had taken three days to get an audience with her and a day for her to make up her mind. But at last she had said to him, "Bring me this Gray Wanderer, that I may see her for myself." And that, of course, was how I was named.

So I was brought before her, the Queen from whose own body should have sprung the next rulers. Only she was girl-barren. Her many princes plowed her, but there was no harvest. She had no girl children to grieve her, only boys. She did not know when I came to her that her bearing days were already over and that her sister's son would rule after her.

But we did not know all that would transpire then. The Queen asked to see me out of simple curiosity and because the news was brought by a beautiful young man.

I dressed, as was appropriate to my age and clan, in a long gray homespun gown pricked through with red and black and green embroidery. I had done it myself, the trillis twined around the boughs and a sprinkling of mourning berries along the hem. My mother called it fine, my grandmother complained of the stitchery.

My hair was plaited and pinned upon my head. My grandmother thought it silly to travel that way, my mother said it was best to have it off my neck. I thought them both crazed to argue about my looks. I had never been any great beauty, but a great gawking girl a head taller than the rest.

They agreed on one thing, though.

"Stand tall," my mother said, pulling at the sides of my dress.

"Pride in bearing can make the difference," added my grandmother, fussing with my hair.

I assumed they began quarreling again as soon as I left, and to tell the truth for many long years I missed the sound of their banter. It was never quarreling in anger, but a kind of conversation between the two of them, statement and response, as predictable and satisfying as an antiphonal poem.

Because they had asked it of me, I held my head high, though I took the braids down as soon as we were out of sight. It was too heavy for the long trip piled up that way.

What happened along the road I forget, though I know I wanted B'oremos to turn and talk to me. But he was intent on finding the quickest way there.

And when we arrived at the great city of L'Lal'dome, with the twin towers marking the place like gigantic stone arrows, I was suddenly too frightened and too homesick to react. So I kept to the silence that B'oremos had begun.

When the Queen saw me, she smiled. I was so young, she told me later, and so serious she could not help but smile at me. She smiled as most Royals do, more lips than teeth, but widely.

"Come, child," she said, leaning forward and holding out her hand.

I did not know any better and took it, oblivious to the mutterings around me, and that marked the beginning of our strange friendship. Then I leaned forward and whispered so that she alone could hear it. "Do not fear the dark, my lady, for I am sent to light your way."

It was not the speech I had practiced with my mother, nor yet the one my grandmother had made me promise to recite. Nor was it the one I had made up along the way as I traipsed behind B'oremos hoping he would turn and speak to me. But when I saw the Queen with the grief of all those girl-barren years sitting above her eyes, I knew why I had come. B'oremos was just a pretty thing, a toy forgot. It was to serve *this* Queen and our land that I was there. So I spoke those words to her; not for the applause of the court or to turn B'oremos's head, but for the Queen alone. And because I did it that way, she knew I was speaking the truth.

She bade me sit at her feet, perched on the lowest cushion of Queenship. I thought I would never leave.

Then she asked to see my grief poems and I took the first of the Gray Wanderer ones from the carry-basket. They are in the Queen's Hall now, behind locked doors, where only the scholars can read them, but once they had been set out for everyone to see.

She read them with growing interest and called up the white-robed priestesses to her.

"A child of Lands shall lead the way," the priestess said cryptically, rubbing her hands along the sides of her robe. They always speak thus, I have found, leaving a leader many paths to choose from. Grievers and priestesses have this elliptical speech in common, I think, though the priestesses would claim True Knowledge and Infallibility while I can only speak in symbols what I feel here, here in the heart.

The Queen nodded and turned to me. "And can you make me another threnody? Now? Now, while I watch, so that I can see that you made these without the promptings of your elders?"

I said what I then believed. "I have no one to grieve for, my Queen."

She smiled.

In those days, remember, I was young and from a small village and a Minor Hall. What did I know of Queens? I thought it was a pitying smile. I know better now. It was a smile of power.

Several days later word came that my grandmother had died and I had much to grieve for then. I wondered what my mother would do without someone to argue with, whether she would become a silent husk herself. But I was not allowed to go home to do my grieving or to offer myself as the other tongue to my mother's lost duet. No, the Queen herself set me up at a table in a Major Hall and on that stage, surrounded by the sophisticated mourners of the court, I began my public life. I wrote thirteen threnodies in the seven days and composed a master lament, though I should not have had the skill. My grief was fed by homesickness and by the image of my mother struck dumb by grief.

> Grief was the gag that silenced her,
> She never sang again.

That was really about my mother, and it turned out to be true.

I had those hardened mourners weeping within a day. The Queen herself had to take to bed out of grief for my grandmother, though the strangest thing was that I had never realized before how much the old woman had meant to me.

The Queen called the best grievers in the land to teach me in relays after the Seven was up. Within the year I knew as much as they of the history of mourning, the structure of threnodies, and the composition of the dirge. I learned the Queen's birth lines to twice the twenty-one names and the lines of her cousins as well. I held in my mouth and mind the first of the hundred prime tales and was already beginning on their branches. What I learned I did not forget. And when I had Mastery conferred on me, I stood in the Room of Instruction with the other apprentices and had the tale of the Seven Grievers given to me. All this, which usually takes half a lifetime, I learned in a year.

And for a night I had a prince as a lover, though I never bore him a babe.

But I see a question in your eyes, child. Do not be afraid to ask. Wait, let me ask it for you. Did I regret my years of service to the Queen when I learned that she had had my grandmother slain? Child, you have lived all your life with the knowledge of the strangers from the sky. You are one of the changed grievers. We did not question a Queen. She did what she did for the good of our land. I do what I do for the good of my art. My grandmother's lines were long and full of Royal mourners; her dying was short and without pain. Would that we could all start our journey that way.

It was proclaimed by the Queen, and approved by the priestesses, that a Master Griever of the Queen's own choosing—though she be not a birth-rite griever—could mourn the Queen and hers. It was a first change in what would become a time full of change. Thus it was that I served the Queen and her sister's son after. Who is mourned does not matter to the Master Griever; we mourn for men and women alike. But I see now that it is, in the end, the land that mourns. I fear it will become as barren as my Queen. For who can tell which man is father when all men sow the same? Yet a woman in her time of ripening is each as different as a skillfully wrought dirge.

I know not if the land will die because of the King or the strangers. Tall and broad they are, easy to admire and touch. They show us wonders, their tongues invent tales, they are a people without tears. Do not trust them unless you see them cry. It is the one thing beyond their magics.

Their magics are easy and magic, like art, should be tough, should make demands. They give and give until we are caught in the net of their giving. And what do they ask in return? It seems a simple enough demand: that we talk to them that they may capture our words with their machines. The Queen has ruled and the priestess agrees that this does not violate the prophesies. The machines do not script the words but capture the voice. Yet is it not said in the first prime tale that to hold in the mouth is to re-member? A machine has no mouth. A machine has no heart. We are nothing if we forget our own tales.

Things change too quickly for me, my child. But remember what you promised. You said you would set out my husk on the pyre and pylons we built together, hand on hand, outside this cave, so far away from the palace and the troubled streets of L'Lal'dome. I should not be too heavy for you to lift—now.

Here, listen, I have made up a threnody of my own, the first Gray Wanderer I have composed in many years—and the last. I want you to start my mourning with it. It begins:

> Gray is my color and my name,
> Fame is the morning's mourning . . .

My voice falters. You sing it. I know, I know you have not the tidiest voice in the land. It is little like the voice of a bird that has sucked the juice of too many sun-warmed berries. But, Grenna, I want *you* to say this for me. Oh, I know such is not done, that a griever grieve for herself. But I have no child of my womb, no girl to call the lines.

But what of Linnet?

She is a child of the sky, none of ours. *I*, I am the last of the Lania, though once I had different hopes. And even though you are my chosen one, it is not the same, no matter what the Queen once proclaimed. I am ever drawn back to the old ways, away from the sky-farers' lovely lies. Even in my dying I must be the Gray Wanderer. Say the words:

> Gray is my color and my name,
> Fame is the morning's mourning . . .

Bring me my last meal now and the Cup of Sleep. I will rest for a moment. The pain is great today and my head swirls with darkness. You will make them remember me, will you not? The threnody is written down, but once you have it, destroy the writing. To hold it in the mouth is to remember. You *will* make them remember me? Say it. Say it. Do not cry. Crying does not become the griever.

May your time of dying be short.

Good. And may your own lines of grieving be long. Now paint your eyelids for me, but lightly. Pinch your cheeks for color. You will?

I will.

Good. And may your time of dying be short, too. Now, my beloved only child, go.

Tape 3:

THE SINGER
OF DIRGES

Place: *Palace of the King, Apartment of King*

Time: *King's Time 1, First Patriarchy; labtime 2137.5 + A.D.*

Speaker: *the King, called B'oremos, also called the Singer of Dirges to Anthropologist Aaron Spenser*

Permission: *King's own*

She never believed in her own beauty, but it was that which first drew me to her. In that small and terrible Hall, with the lines of mourners weeping over the most ordinary of griefs, she caught the eye. Even before I read her words and knew them for the lost words of all my songs, even before that I could not help but be drawn to her.

She was tall, like a Royal, and had a natural willowy grace beneath the artifices she had adopted for her first public grieving. Never awkward in public, she seemed rather unaware of the eyes on her. I liked that. However I never liked those painted nails, the ones with the crosses scratched into the coloring. They always looked like dead nails to me, of a corpse long lying on the pylon after the birds have eaten the softer parts. Of course my fellow Royals took them up with a fervor they often reserved for such grotesqueries. It is to Gray's credit, though, that she found those passions amusing and gave up the carvings of her nails long before the rest. Perhaps she did it because I found it distasteful

27

and told her so. I would like to think that she did something because of me, though as a man of that time I was only on the periphery of her thoughts.

I had gone to that Hall because it was part of my training. Young men of the Royals have ceremonial duties and my fingers had early found music in the unlikeliest strings. So I was taught to play ten different instruments, from the plecta to the harmonus, and sent—like all male Royals—to practice my youthful skills before audiences in rural Halls. It was an odious mission, though I was always successful. (It is foolish being humble about one's gifts.) I loved to draw folk to me with the power in my voice and the music in my hands, and I must admit that I had a pretty face then, though one might not guess it by looking at me now. A pretty face is common enough coin among Royals. Besides, without my musical gift could I have discovered Gray, who was to become the light that guided me and who—in the end—was the reason for the Cup of Sleep I ever keep at my hand?

But I digress and you grow distracted. You have always been more interested in our customs than in my reveries, more taken by what I represent than in who I long to be. I had best return to the mission year so as to make you understand what it was to be a Royal.

I had been months on the road and learned nothing there. There is nothing to be learned from common folk. I simply sang again and again the old songs which those country grievers never tired of, slipping in the name of a grieven one, relying on the common rhymes. It is a trick of which I am only lately ashamed.

Each stop at a small Hall of Grief, with the un-
imaginative weeping caryatids and the banal deck-
ings of trillis and dark berries and green boughs, the
traditional trappings, brought me success. Each
success brought me enormous suppers and pretty
plump girls to warm my bed. And as I was young
and just trying on my brief manhood, I accepted
such offerings as my Royal and artistic due. I would
not admit to myself that pretty girls can be stamped
out of a mold as coins, and that one can tire of them
equally. It was years before I realized that, as a
young prince, my services were in demand to plow
the fertile country fields for the occasional harvest
of Royals. They used me—and I enjoyed the usage,
never wondering to what end I was employed. I was
foolish, perhaps, to think it all my own doing.

And then I entered that small Hall of Grief,
scarcely distinguished from others before it. It was
in the Middle Lands, where pigs and people shared
houses and nothing new had been thought or written
or sung since the rule of the first Queens. The coast,
where we Royals cluster, is bathed by mutable
waters which—so it is said—accounts for the fact
that the citizens of L'Lal'dome are so amenable to
change. Did we not first invite you sky-farers in?

Invite?

Let us not quarrel like women over words, friend.

It was not a quarrel, but a question.

You sound like our seers, though I know you are
not as seedless as they.

But about your mission year?

Yes, that year. To the Middle Lands at the last.
Of course I had earlier toured through the Rocks or
Homelands (though why they are called that I have
always wondered, since I, certainly, have never felt

at home there). Rocks live in an inhospitable domain and so they and the Moons folk who also dwell there revel in hardy inventions. And many are the people of Arcs and Bow who move to the mountains to practice their skills. In the mountain caves the hardy members of Rocks wrest precarious livings from the precipices and cliff faces. All those folk look at the world aslant, living so long in the dark or dangling at the end of a rope. However it does make their girls all the wilder and their Halls more interesting. Their weeping statues cry real gems.

But the people of the Middle are fat and contented, wallowing in their complacencies as their pigs in mud.

Did I say I hated my mission year? I hated being *there*, in Lands, at the end of my journeying, and I counted the days until I had sung in every Lands Hall and could be gone.

And then I saw her and everything was changed for me. Slim where the others were plump, bony where they were rounded, she was Royal sown, of that there was no doubt. Her long blue-black hair had been braided so tightly the skin by her eyes was stretched, giving her the startled look of a young creature in flight. The sticky berries plaited into her hair seemed a warning that she was not to be touched without consequences. She was, in fact, the only girl at that Hall I did not caress. The dying trillis caught 'round the plait only emphasized her fragility, though I was to learn later that she could be as tough and as unmovable and as unforgiving as any Queen.

I had been asked to sing under the sign of a local harper, I think it was. He had died a scant month or two before and they were still eager to grieve for

him. I trotted out some of the great old songs to
begin with, songs that had always brought tears to
the Royals: "Dirge for the Dying Sun," "The
Waters of L'Lal'ladia," and "Threnody for a Princess Dying Young." That was to get their attention,
to draw the crowds in. Then I sang several impro-
vised lyrics in the old style, weaving in the harper's
name and the few honest facts about his life I had
gleaned from his mourning kin. Of course when I
stopped for a draught of wine—that unrefined in-
ferior grape residue they passed off as drinkable
there—the crowds began to wander away. Lands
folk are easy to please but have short memories.
That is why making love to their girls brings no last-
ing pleasure.

When the lines for the harper had dissipated—
and I was glad to have them go, as it meant short-
ening my stay—and I had been praised sufficiently
by the harper's folk for the moment or two of immortality I had brought to him, I left. My duty done,
I could wander the aisles seeing if—once again—I
would learn nothing from the grievers in a Lands
Hall.

The crush of signs—complacent pig, contented
cow, befuddled hen, rolling millstone, upright pitch-
fork, leaning harp—replicated the crush of mourners who touched shoulders without really touching
grief. So shallow were their concerns they cried
equally at the old banalities of a teller who borrowed
a hoary tale as at the tears of a young griever sobbing
about her sister dead only a day. Imagine not being
able to distinguish art from artifice. The ordinari-
ness of the Hall abused my senses, and besides, I
was becoming hungry. I started toward the door and
was already calculating where my next stop would

be, an even smaller Hall marked on the map as Pigton after its main inhabitants, one supposed, when
I saw her.

She was sitting and writing, but even sitting she
seemed tall. And the combination of fragility and
strength flowed from her in waves. She was bent
over a tablet shaping the words with her mouth first
before writing them down. The table around her was
uncluttered, which distinguished it immediately
from the others. I had to stop and look at it.

Without thinking, I muttered the first of the ritual
words, gesturing at the memoria so artfully placed.
"I would have liked them."

She looked up and her eyes, that amber opalesc-
ence of the finest gemstones that marked her further
as Royal sown, stared into mine. Unlike the weak
blue eyes of the common grievers, hers did not shim-
mer with unshed tears and it was thus I saw, for the
first time, her inner strength. She shed tears, but
only when deeply moved.

Her voice was low, slow, so different from the
high giggling inanities of the other girls. She said
simply, "They would have grown by your friendship." It took me a moment to remember that was
the ordinary rote of grieving, the ritual response to
my own ritual words.

Then she looked down again at the linen on which
she had been writing, not coyly in order to keep me
by her side, but because she had something more
important to do than gaze into the desire-filled eyes
of a princeling. She pulled the linen free of the
stretcher, a trick of her own devising, and I was
forced to put my hand out to flatten the cloth so as
to read what she had scripted.

It would not have mattered at that moment if what she had written was as banal as the rest of the Hall. I was caught up in her differences and would have read them into anything she wrote. She was as unlikely a Lands woman as I had ever met. She could have been a Queen. That is heresy, I know. But I am King now. Anything I say is true.

But what I read on that linen was as startling as she, a perfect little piece of poetry that could not possibly have been written by a mere Middle girl. It was simple, unsophisticated, direct. The words were mostly one syllable, the images spare. It even gained power read aloud, for its sounds were as strong and steady and unflinching as funerary drums.

First I only spoke the poem over and over. Then I began to sing it, improvising tunes that were, in the beginning, too ornate a setting for the words, too derivative of the classical melodies. At last the words began to dictate a series of melodic phrases, the melodies constricted to a single modal tune. It was unforgettable, with a chorus that was soon ringing through the Hall.

I have never since written such a fine song, though I have constructed thousands of them, many to Gray's own words; but it is enough that I wrote the one.

Do you want to continue?
Of course. I will take just a sip of wine. Old age dries the tongue.

I could not stay, of course. And the rest of my mission to Pigton and beyond were forgot. All those minor Minor Halls would have to do without my

singing and my sowing. Besides, there were other
Royals on their way—L'eoninanos and G'al'ladinos
were some weeks behind me, the one a poet and the
other possessor of a fine magical hand. They would
draw the crowds and the girls with equal ease. But
I could not stay because the hope of the mission
year, beyond learning about our people—or from
them, a *forlorn* hope—was the charge: Reap the
Harvest. For we Royals sow often though we gather
a meager crop. Once in many years there is a prodigy like Gray, though more often it is that a year of
gazing at sheep makes a single ewe attractive. But
I could not chance it. I had to return to L'Lal'dome.

I bought an animal to ride; spavined and sway-
backed as it was, it was all the town could spare.
The coin I used was my own body. I was quick, and
I can't imagine the girl or her mother had any pleasure in the exchange. I certainly did not. But the
horse they sold me compensated them in the long
run, for it bruised me in private places and coughed
great globules of sputum on my boots whenever we
stopped, and it died messily on the second day in a
patch of bellywort. I was hours after picking the
thorns from my clothes. Still, the beast saved me a
day of walking, and for that I was grateful to the
girl, to her tight-fisted mother, and to the beast itself, for which I composed a short and rather bawdy
grief quarto. I made it back to the court in three
days instead of the expected four.

After months on the road, lying on the straw-
stuffed mattresses offered by the six Common
Grievers and eating their swill, it was a pleasure just
to look at the wide cobbled roads leading into
L'Lal'dome. The turrets of the palace rose before
me, dominating the landscape: the left-hand tower

with its juts and precipices, the right-hand tower
with its smooth glissades. We call them the sky
twins, and they are an unlikely pair. It is said they
were built by two quarreling princesses, both of
whom hoped to be Queen. The towers were completed but the princesses died young, ending their
particular line. The Queens who followed kept the
towers as reminders of false hopes.

I was delighted to see the imposing pair, a signal
that I was home. I wondered what Gray would say
when I brought her here. Would she start with delight at the differences between the twins? Or would
she silently compose an ode comparing them to
some grieven sister or aunt? Would the cobble
stones amuse her—or merely bruise her country
feet?

Lost in similar rehearsals, I made my way
through the twisting market streets to the Apartments of Princes, where I knew a hot bath would
be ready.

Plumbing is the prerogative of Royals. We have
the water and the wisdom, drawn from the comple-
ment of Stars who first devised the system of pipes
and weirs. For the sharing of their knowledge and
the skill of their hands, we allow the folk of Stars
to live alongside us in L'Lal'dome as partners,
though not, of course, as equals. But we rarely in-
termingle. It is considered bad form for a princeling
to ally with a girl from Stars; besides, they are a
boring folk, stiff-necked and overserious. Of course
a Queen can always choose to lie with whom she
will.

But I gave solemn thanks that day—as I had
never done before—to the anonymous Stars who

had invented the baths. It was worth all the dirty traveling in the Middle Lands to come home to the pleasure of hot water and soap.

The bath room was crowded when I arrived, crowded with servers as well as my fellow princes. As I stripped for the warming pool, leaving my mission clothes (ugly, worn, common things) in a pile, I was hooted at by T'arremos.

"He's gotten thin and wan. Perhaps he dies of too much touching—poor, dirty bardling."

A grimace was my only answer. T'arremos was always slight in wit and ill-favored as well. He had a birth scar, a bold berry-colored mark like a map on one side of his face. Because of it his mission year had been singularly unsuccessful. He had had to *buy* the favors of what few girls he could find and he had only once been chosen to serve the Queen. His failures were public ones and they flavored his speech with a permanent sourness.

Ignoring T'arremos, I slipped into the pool, letting the warm water lave me. I resisted the urge to duck under. Such a display would have been bad form indeed.

T'arremos tried again. "Home early. We thought you were to be gone another month. The girls of Middle Lands too much for you then? Or did they forget to applaud your performances?"

I resisted the immediate response, sensing that there were some princes there who were as jealous as T'arremos at my successes with the plecta and harmonus. Instead, I stood up, leaving the warmth of the pool before being truly centered in it, and turned slowly toward him. I showed him, without words, that I—unlike he—was a well-favored Royal still in my prime. Then, even more slowly, and smiling, I said, "I am home early for there is one the Queen must see."

I stepped gracefully from the pool and walked— not exactly strutting but only a fine line away from it—to the heated pool beyond where I stretched up on my toes, raised my arms above my head, and dove in. I stayed under for as long as I could, then surfaced, careful not to breathe heavily, though my chest ached and I longed to gulp in the water-laden air.

As I had hoped, the whole bath room was abuzz with my statement and T'arremos was gone. He had, I hoped, raced out to tell one of his Masters, for he often spied for the older princes, those closest to the Queen. And *they* were the ones who could help me get an early audience with her. But it would have been no good trying a direct approach with them. They loved intrigue and I would have had to waste days. That T'arremos, too, would be favored in this exchange was a necessary evil that I planned to sort out afterward. First, though, I had to make myself clean.

More wine?
Thank you. I see my memoirs do not bore you.
On the contrary, they are fascinating.
Do not patronize me, sky-farer. The King knows everything.
And will, I hope, tell all in his own good time.
What I will tell may not be all, but it will be the truth.

My rooms, with their silken draperies and soft-filtered light, were exactly as I had left them nearly three seasons before. The walls, covered with my collection of ancient viols, welcomed me home. Still naked from the baths, I wandered from instrument to instrument, strumming and plucking, a ritual I had devised as a child to help my thinking. Certain dominant chords centered my thoughts, certain arpeggios lent permission for flights of fancy. My servants knew better than to intrude on either my practicing or my thinking. Though they might listen, they would never enter until the run of strings was done or until I called them into my presence. A well-trained servant is one of life's greatest pleasures.

We do not believe in servants.

Neither do the Common Grievers, though many of them move to L'Lal'dome to serve us. And do you not serve your chief?

It is not the same.

No, it is never the same.

I sat down on a plush pillow, one of the eight I was allowed, crossed my legs, and pulled my favorite plecta onto my lap. It had an old autumn-colored box of smooth wood. The body arched deeply and the sounding boards were intricately inlaid with decorated ivories worked from the bones of small animals. The neck was fretted which indicated how old it was. The sound post was also of bone, giving it a richer, fuller tone than if made of wood. I had purchased that particular plecta for its dark resonances and had polished it with a honey-wax the long chilly winter of my thirteenth year. The other princes had laughed at my dedication to a single worn instrument. Indeed, T'arremos had called it an *obsession.* Of course the other princes who played mostly preferred the newer multicolored viols from the Rock Street merchants. But using this ancient plecta is more than an affectation with me, though I would not call it an obsession. I have a real love for the old unpainted strings. They echo, they sound the centuries, just as we older princes do. You see, I still call myself a prince, though I have had the thirty cushions for almost a year.

But I apologize, I stray far from my tale. You want to know about the Gray Wanderer, you said, not some old prince whose organs shriveled up years ago and whose sole pleasures are in the stewardship of state, small pieces of gossip, and memories.

Well, I played Gray's song over and over on my plecta, teaching my mind to remember what my fingers already easily recalled. I was able to embroider the tune a bit, for the strings were wonderfully supple on this instrument, though I had not plucked it for three seasons past. (I had carried only a worn harmonus for my travels.)

The song echoed in the room till the very walls were party to Gray's great-grandmother's immortality. And when I was satisfied that I would not stumble when presenting the song to the Queen, I stood. Gazing out of the window into the courtyard below I was surprised to find that it was already dark.

"Mar-keshan," I called out and my servant entered immediately.

He was old and brown as cow spittle, but I would not let him retire. He had been old when he had come into my service on my birth day. He was, in fact, so old that his blue eyes were practically translucent, yet still—I think—they saw more truly than any of the young servers I have around me today.

"My lord," he said, bowing, showing no surprise at my early return or any indication that I had been gone months without a word to him.

"I will eat and then be dressed," I said. "Any requests for me?"

"The Prince D'oremos would see you this evening at your leisure." He allowed himself a part smile because he knew what such an invitation meant. Mar-keshan had been a server for enough years to understand princely politics well, though he was originally only a Waters man who chose service instead of the sea.

I smiled back at him. Understand—only in the privacy of my apartment would I ever do such a thing. It is bad form to be intimate with your servants. But Mar-keshan was more than a servant. He was my oldest—well, *friend* may be too strong a word, but we knew each other well. We said nothing, though. One never knows what holes have been bored behind the curtains to allow for listening ears.

I signed to him with the hand signals we had long ago adopted: This is interesting and we shall talk of it later. Then I said, aloud, "I will eat first," and sent him away with another wave of my hand. He left quietly and I made one more tour of the strings, plucking, strumming, bowing. It was good, indeed, to be home.

D'oremos had an apartment with five rooms, each larger than my entire holding. Though he no longer lay with the Queen—indeed, how could he, being over fifty years, his organs drawn back up since the end of his prime—he was her first adviser. If she listened to anyone, she listened to him. And it was said he still pleasured her in other ways, but I knew she preferred the company of sweet-breathed princes and an occasional muscular girl from the ranks of Arcs and Bow.

I had been to his room only twice before. The first time was when I had turned thirteen and he had asked to hear my songs. I had been playing at a master level for three years, then, an unusual circumstance. He had heard me often at the conserts where I had been something of a prodigy. There I usually played in groups, with small solos. But my reputation had grown steadily and this intimate recital for the chief of the princes would put the cap on it. I played for him.

He had lain among his pillows, stroking the long waterfalls of his mustaches as I performed. I cannot recall the tunes, but I know that I brought three instruments with me: the violetta, because he had requested it; the verginium, because I was the only one who regularly played it with any facility; and, of course, my sonorous plecta.

He said nothing when I was done but waved a languid hand, which his servants interpreted correctly as a call for food. I was too nervous to eat but began instead to babble about music. He silenced me with another wave of his hand and finished his small meal of succulents without a word. A servant appeared with a bowl of scented water. D'oremos washed his hands and mustache, then dried them with a rainbow-colored cloth.

When the servant left, D'oremos turned to me, his hard marble eyes staring into mine. "Your music moved me deeply," he said, though there was no clue to it in his voice. Then he leaned back against his pillows and closed his eyes.

After a moment, I realized the audience was at an end. I rose, careful to silence the plecta's strings with my palm, shouldered the other two instruments, and left.

The second time he was no warmer, but at least he spoke more. It was two years later when my organs had descended and I was about to go out on my mission year. Since he was the official Father of Princes, at the Queen's own appointment, it was his duty to inform each prince in turn of the Rites of Sowing.

He was brusque in his explanations, having me strip and using my body as the template for his talk. Much of what he told me I had learned already in the vernacular, in giggling embraces with L'eoninanos and G'al'ladinos in the baths or at night when we fumbled in wine-fogged attempts to draw one another's immature organs out. But there was much that was new as well, for I had never lain with a woman. That was for the mission year. And I learned from D'oremos that night the secret of the Royals: of the short years we have to sow and why there is so little reaping done. It could have been a painful discovery had he chosen to make it so. But his dry explication made it seem no more than a minor burden, a small payment for the many and varied pleasures of being a Royal. I accepted it without tears as a prince should. Grieving, after all, is an art, not an indulgence.

But this third invitation was of a different sort. Though I had not completed a full year of sowing, though I still had four or five good years to plow our Queen, I was considered a man, to be summoned, as a man is summoned, to D'oremos's quarters. I went, plecta slung across my back, fast enough to show him that I was willing to partner him in this venture; slow enough to indicate that I did not plan to bend to his will.

He opened the door himself, an indication of the importance he attached to our meeting, though he

smiled me no greeting. I matched his control, merely
nodding my head, the young prince to his father.

He gestured to a set of ten pillows. *Ten* pillows!
It was better than I had hoped. I set the plecta on
the floor and sank back against the pillows, waiting.

He lay back on his twenty cushions and stroked
the long graying strands of his mustache before
speaking. "You are home before time. I will not
insult your intelligence or mine with games. Tell me
what you have to tell me and then we will eat."

I had thought to make a long, convoluted tale of
it, with choice anecdotes about the plump and pretty
girls I had met and my successes in the Halls. And
if it had been the other major prince, C'arrademos,
such a ploy would have worked well. But one look
at D'oremos's face stayed me. I was direct with him.

"In a minor Lands Hall I met a girl. Her name
is Lina-Lania. She is tall, yellow-eyed, slim, and in
her first Hall has written a poem that is like no other
I have ever heard. It has simple grace and is the
most moving thing . . ." I stopped.

"You sound like a fool made from tumbling,"
D'oremos said. He said it without rancor or judgment. It was a simple statement.

"I would not ally with a Middle Lands girl,
though I might tumble her," I said. "But her words
fit my songs, the songs I have not yet written, the
ones I am meant to write."

He did not answer.

"We were told to look for Royals begat in earlier
sowings. *You* told me, in this very room. *Reap the
Harvest*." My voice took on a slightly petulant tone.

Still he did not speak.

"Lina-Lania is one. I am sure of it."

He looked up at the ceilings, which were draped
in red-and-gold silks. Without meaning to, my eyes

followed his. The corner of one silk had pulled away
from its fastening and drooped slightly. D'oremos
clicked his tongue against the roof of his mouth, a
small deadly warning, and I knew that there was a
servant who would be given the choice of the Cup
or dismissal come morning.

"I also was certain I had found one," he mused.
"The next year she grew fat on Royal food and I
realized that her yellow eyes were only a muddy
reflection of a boy's desire. She did not last long
and took the Cup willingly." He smiled at the memory. "She was a pretty thing, for a while."

I was silent.

"T'arremos brought back twin boys, and you
know how rarely there are twins born. Perhaps once
every three of four generations. They were mar-
velous children. Very inventive physically, but stupid beyond belief. Even the Queen laughed at T'arremos. He sent them home, denying them the last
comfort of the Royal Cup. We are, I fear, breeding
fewer and fewer." He pulled on one side of his mustache, which gave his face a lopsided, quizzical
expression. "How sure are you?"

I reached out for the instrument, my eyes never
leaving his, and brought the plecta onto my lap. It
was such a wonderful, sturdy old thing and I knew
it would need no further tuning, which would have
spoiled the moment. I played the Gray Wanderer's
song.

On the second time through, D'oremos's thin,
reedy tenor, slightly off-key, joined me in the chorus:

> Weep for the night that is coming,
> Weep for the day that is past.

Tears began to leak from his eyes, down the well-worn grooves in his face. I had not expected that. My fingers slowed to a stop.

"My father," I whispered.

"She shall have her audience with the Queen," he said, leaned back against his pillows, and closed his eyes.

I waited a minute more, hoping to hear the terms of our mutual undertaking. Then, understanding that there would be no demands from him, that finding Lina-Lania was enough, I rose and went back to my rooms.

I should have celebrated, I suppose, celebrated both my return to the comforts of L'Lal'dome and the success of my shortened mission. But I felt strangely cold and sick at heart. I slipped out of my robes and lay in the darkness, pressed against my eight pillows.

Mar-keshan came and went several times on quiet feet. He left bowls of sweet-smelling fruit to tempt me and slipped two new pillows under my head.

"Sent from Lord D'oremos," he said, pride in his voice.

But I could not eat and I could not sleep, though I must have dozed off in the end, for I dreamed that a gray-cloaked figure stood at my feet, carefully away from the cushions, and offered me a cup of blood, crying all the while I drank.

We shall speak of this again tomorrow.

Tape 4:

THE SEVEN GRIEVERS, PART II

Place: *Queen's Hall of Grief, Room of Instruction*
Time: *Queen's Time 23, Thirteenth Matriarchy;
        labtime 2132.5 + A.D.*
Speaker: *Queen's Own Griever to the apprentices,
          including Lina-Lania*
Permission: *No permission, preset, voice-
            activated*

And here continues the song of the Seven Grievers
as was told Master to Master down through the lines
from the hour of the waters receding to the moment
of my tongue's speaking. I have saved these mourn-
ful dirges in my mouth and in my heart for the time
when, as the Queen's Own Griever, I have had to
wail for the dying of the land once more.

Hear then, listen well. My word is firm, firmer
than sleep or the Cup that carries it, firmer than the
strength of heroes. My voice makes the telling true.
To listen, to remember, is to know.

Onto the great crescent that was once the floor
of the sea moved Lands and with them the folk of
Moons and Stars, those who sowed no grain and
grew no corn but reaped a harvest of words.

> **Moons**, the white-kirtled seers who
> with lavia and chronium chart the
> warm winds and cold, who chronicle
> the seasons and count forth the falling

rain, who with rood and orb prophesy
the end of one life, the beginning of
another.

Stars, who carry knowledge in their
hands as well as their heads, who
script the histories of Queens and track
their lines, but whose words are barren
of immortality or art.

Then from the ranks of Lands and Waters,
Rocks, Moons, and Stars there arose a hardy, foolish few.

"Why must we live like cattle, browsing on the
tillage of the soil," they cried, "captive of the winds
and storms that worry the fields? Give us red meat
that we snare from the teeming forests, that we trap
with the cunning that is in our hands."

And they ran off into the woods to hunt and fight
and live like beasts. There they tempered their anger
with hunger and tempered their hunger with fear,
for in the woods they were both feeder *and* fed on,
and many fell to the cunning of fang and claw. These
runners were known first as Hunters and later as
Arcs and Bow, and for many years they set themselves apart from the rest. Though they were all
children of the Night-Seers—sturdy, stout, and
low—they came not near their kin but bred with
their own. They bore many children, though most
died young.

Then one arose from the ranks of Arcs and Bow,
a great hunter and a mother of girls, who saw farther
than the tops of the trees that kept them prisoned,
who saw more deeply than the deepest hunting pits.

"Why do we not live, one upon another, trading our red meat for the yellow grain, sharing with our long cousins the bounty of forest and field?"

And from that time, Arcs and Bow joined again with their cave kin. They were like sisters under one roof, quarreling, who separate for a time and then come together again in their mother's house to celebrate the seasons and the harvesting of days.

Selah.

Tape 5:

PRINCE OF TRAITORS

Place: *Palace of the King, Apartment of King*

Time: *King's Time 1, First Patriarchy; labtime*
2137.5 + A.D.

Speaker: *the King, called B'oremos, also called*
the Singer of Dirges to Anthropologist
Aaron Spenser

Permission: *King's own*

I betrayed her three times.

Do you want to begin that way?

It is our custom, sky-farer, to let a person tell his story in his own style, neither judging nor questioning. Is your recorder set?

It is.

Then forget it. It will do what it must do. But you must learn to listen.

I will listen.

I betrayed her three times. I thought each a loving act. I did it for the Queen and, perhaps, I did it for myself. It brought me here, to the thirty cushions of Kingship which I hold until the time there is a princess old enough to ascend the throne. And it brought me as well to the Cup of Sleep. Truly it is said, "Kick at the world, break your own foot." I limp and thus I learn. But had I to do it over, there would still have been only the one way. Though I might have understood it better, I would have betrayed her again. The Queen demanded it and I followed the Queen's way.

On the second morning after my meeting with D'oremos, there came a message from him that said quite simply: "Bring the girl."

51

I left at once, neglecting to carry even the plecta with me, though the lack of any instrument riding between my shoulders was heavier than if one had been there. I took one of D'oremos's riding beasts, for this was not a mission trip where every stone in the path and every straw mattress along the way is to leave its impression upon the body of a prince. I was—this time—on an errand direct from the Queen. And, as we were all reminded, "Queen's time is now!"

The beast was a fat slug given to long lunches, but riding it was quicker than walking on my own. I stayed in none of the towns along the way, preferring a celibate blanket in a meadow sweet with windstrife and the heavy musk of night-blooming moons' cap. I guess I wanted to find Gray without the prints of hands on my body or the bruises of mouths on mine. I had been washed clean by my stay in L'Lal'dome and I wanted to remain that way.

Certainly it made for early starts. Each morning began with a streaky sunrise, birdsong, and the tiny snip-snap of the moons' caps closing. I prayed for strength, for courage in the woods, for the mind-set of a girl from Arcs and Bow. I fear I was sadly lacking in woods' grace or the nuances of the hunt and I had neglected, in my eagerness to be on my way, to take the bag of bread and cheese that Markeshan had left out for me. By the time I entered Gray's small holdings, I was starved for both food and conversation. A few nuts and berries (I know at least *that* much about the forest) and a sluggish steed fed neither hunger well.

I rode right up to the Hall of Grief, which had not improved in my absence, and left the horse outside. I wondered again that such a catastrophe of

commonplaces as this town could have produced
that startling willowy girl.

Inside, the usual cries and wailings could be
heard, and a tune or two of such stifling unoriginality
that I fear I yawned as I searched for her. It was a
yawn lent strength by my nights in the woods. I
covered my mouth as I looked around. A prince
needs to remember his manners.

As a Royal, I am a head taller than the Lands
folk, something you strangers—taller even than
we—will have noticed. So one sweep of the Hall
convinced me Gray was not there.

I made my way to the table under the millstone
sign.

"The girl," I said. "Lina-Lania. Where is she?"

A sallow-faced, blue-eyed boy with dark hair like
a curtain over his forehead, stared up at me. He was
slack-jawed, uncomprehending.

"Your sister-cousin, Lina-Lania."

"Linni?"

The idiot knew his kin only by a family pet name,
and a name which so ill suited her I fear I snorted
at him. He jumped back. What could one do with
such a mentality but rule it?

"Is Linni the tall one?"

He nodded slowly as the answer came to him.
"You want Stick-legs? She's at the mill."

Without a word more—he deserved nothing better—I turned. I would not give him the satisfaction
of even a public touch and I made sure the rest of
the crowd noticed the dismissal. He would be
taunted for that for a good while. I walked straight
out the door.

Since mills are always on the east of a village and
along the waterway, I did not have a difficult search.

The millhouse squatted like a stone beast over the race, its wheel dipping in and out of the water in noisy rotation. That sound would accompany my stay and later I put it in the song cycle of the Gray Wanderer.

I have heard it.

You are supposed to say, "I would have liked her."

And you would answer, "She would have grown by your friendship."

You have learned our ways well, sky-farer.

I did not learn them fast enough.

You have not said whether you enjoyed my songs.

Can one not, *like a King's song?*

I was a musician long before I was a King. I want the truth.

The songs brought Lina-Lania back to life for me.

Is that your way of saying . . .

I loved her? Yes.

No, no, you must say, "I would have *liked* her," not, "I loved her." We do not know the word *love* except in your own tongue. There are different degrees of liking: a friend, a child, a Queen, a night's tumble. "I would have *liked*" is the beginning of ritual and relationship. Say it.

That, too.

Then my grief songs worked. Did you notice the sonority of the drone strings of the plecta? That was the mill's sound. Except for my first song with her, this cycle is my bid for immortality. As long as it is played, she—and I—will be remembered.

I will certainly remember.

Good . . . Then I will tell you the rest, for there is much more to be added to your memory. Your

understanding of what occurred is sadly incomplete.
Of course, we say here on L'Lal'lor that in every
experience there is one to live it and one to tell it.

I have heard that bit of wit before.

Good, then you are prepared to listen well.

*My King, that is what I have been trained for
fully half of my life—and all of yours.*

Then I will continue.

The millhouse was low and crowded with heavy
dark wooden furnishings. Tables and chairs vied for
the center of the one main room. An alcove under
the loft stairs held several buttressed cupboards
carved with deathheads and weeping women. The
room was ringed with curtained beds. Privacy here
was a matter of the imagination. It was like most of
the country houses I had visited along my way.
Even in Lina-Lania's house I longed for the light of
L'Lal'dome.

Gray herself answered my knock. She looked
straight at me, eyes level with mine, but did not
smile. She must have been surprised to see me, but
she did not show it, did not giggle and mince and
touch me the way her Lands kin had done over and
over in every small town I had visited on my mission. It made me favor her the more.

She nodded her head slightly and stepped aside.
I walked in. Her mother and her mother's mother,
both short and squat and dirt-colored, sat at the
table preparing food for the dinner meal and arguing.
They rose on seeing me, their eyes and mouths apol-
ogizing simultaneously.

I took the cleanest chair, the one farthest from
the raw food. I am afraid I wrinkled my nose as they
swept the peelings into a slop pot. Sometimes even

a prince forgoes good manners. But I did nod to
them at the last.

They did not mistake my mission.

"We have been waiting a long time for this discovery," began her mother.

"You have not been waiting. You denied her
prodigy. It was I who first noticed," interrupted the
grandmother.

"The long years have begun to addle you," answered her daughter.

Gray was silent between them.

"There is no one like her in our family," the
grandmother said. Quickly she recited their twenty-
one lines, being three times interrupted by her
daughter. "And never was there one who looked or
sounded like our Linni."

Gray made only a small movement and stared at
the floor. She had always known she had a gift for
grieving, but her body's length had been a torment
to her. Stick-legs, indeed. Children can be cruel.
Even princes. Her shoulders might have rounded
under the burden of their insults; she might have
tried to shrink herself into some kind of easy ac-
ceptance, but she had been too proud to bow under
their tongues.

I walked over to her, put my hand under her chin,
and drew her face up. It was as if she swam up to
me from a great depth, for her eyes pooled with
unshed tears and her mouth trembled somewhere
between a frown and a smile. I felt my own hand
shake with the touch and moved away from her.

"Gray," I whispered, though I am not sure any
of them remarked the significance of the name.

"She is called Lina-Lania," said her mother.

"Linni," insisted her grandmother.

"She will be known as the Gray Wanderer," I said.

Gray smiled at me slowly. And indeed, ever after, she was known to me and mine only by that name.

We started out the next day after I had insulted all of them but Gray by insisting on sleeping in one of the darkly hung beds by myself. The women whispered long into the night about that—and perhaps about other matters as well—but I could not bring myself to tumble any of the brothers or the mother, who was long past childbearing anyway. And to touch Gray here, in the dark, as a duty, was beyond imagining. She would be brought to L'Lal'dome and into the light, where, in the privacy of my rooms, I would clothe her in silken gowns and she would be pleasured like any Royal woman.

She chose the coarsest of Lands gowns for our trip: gray, with embroideries of the rudest sort. With all the beauty of her tongue, she was a five-fingered disaster. The borders of her dress were childishly wrought—red, black, green, with threads carelessly dyed by berry juices. The work was unsophisticated, lacking charm. But she wore the clothes as if they were skins ready to be cast off. I could scarcely wait for her metamorphosis. Under my tutelage this Lands girl would emerge a Royal beauty.

The horse could not carry two, so I left it with the millwife. It was not—as someone suggested later—an ill-conceived payment. Rather I hoped to prolong the trip. Anticipation is one of the best parts of enjoyment. Thinking about a wine is often more satisfying than the first bitter sip. That is why I walked ahead of her much of the way, turning only infrequently to look. Each time I turned back I could savor the glimpses, taste them again and again in my mind.

She hardly spoke as we walked. In fact she was one of the most silent girls I have ever known. Perhaps it came from living with those two quarrelsome women, or perhaps it came from something deeper than that. I did hear her whisper to herself at night but I never asked what it was she said. Somehow her presence, though very satisfying, made me unaccountably shy; I was equally wordless. And without an instrument to hand, I could not sing.

Only once did she share an entire thought with me. It was on the second morning. She had bathed in a pebble-strewn stream unselfconciously. I had spied on her from behind a rock as she splashed cold water across her small breasts. Her hair, shaken loose of the braids, was thick and full down her body and the curling ends were like dark fingers caressing the small of her back. Even after she dressed, I was still trembling from the sight of her and the skin on the backs of my hands and the inside of my thighs ached. But still I did not talk.

She looked at me, almost as if I were not there, and said, "The long years before I came to you were simply a rehearsal; dark passages on either side of a great light."

My knees uncoupled at that and I sat down suddenly, thinking that now, now she would come to me and we would touch, out here in a meadow of windstrife, its silky tendrils being blown over us by a soft breeze. But she walked past me and I was glad that I had not spoken then because I realized that in fact she had not been speaking to me at all. She had been working on a poem, a presentation for the Queen.

I thought about those words more coldly. They were overwrought, childish, dishonest. They were as laughable as her dress.

"We should hurry," I said brusquely, getting up and wiping the windstrife from my clothes.

She nodded, though her eyes, for a moment, looked startled. Then she braided her hair quickly, tying the ends as we walked.

Do you really remember that well?

We pride ourselves on what we hold in the mouth and mind.

Oh.

Besides, my friend, you must not confuse what is actual with what is true.

I am not sure—

What I say now is true. Whether it happened *exactly* that way is not as important as what I am saying. Do you understand? It is important that you understand.

Yes.

Then I will tell you what transpired when we arrived at L'Lal'dome.

As we approached the city the paths became roads, the roads streets, and dirt led into cobbles. She seemed to draw even further into herself. The silence, which had seemed companionable, even sensual before, became an unbridgeable distance between us.

I tried to direct her attention to the twin towers looming ahead. If she saw them, if they meant anything to her, she did not say. She was already well in retreat from me, focusing on the Queen alone. For a moment I was shot through with such jealousies they could scarcely be borne. But my training took over. By squinting my eyes I could make her

into what she was: a tall Lands girls with golden
eyes and an ability to rhyme, nothing more. D'oremos had been right in that.

And so we came to my quarters with silence a
stretched ligature between us. There we were
greeted with high civility by Mar-keshan and my
other servants, but it was Mar-keshan who really
took her in.

He saw in her, he told me years later right before
dying, the haunted look of his sister's daughter. She
had been a very minor sort of griever, taller than
her family and with green-gold eyes. So she had
been taken by a prince to L'Lal'dome. Mar-keshan's confession surprised me. Oh, I had been a
chosen Confessor before and had heard many
strange things that had lain heavily on a man's heart,
blocking his passage into the Light. But I had known
Mar-keshan all my life and had never heard him
mention any family. I had believed that I was all he
had. He had never found his sister's daughter. She
had been discarded and drunk from the Cup a year
before he had gone looking for her. So he took Gray
under his wing, a silent, stubborn protector.

The song I wrote for his passage was a slow dirge
about service; I never mentioned the rest of what
he said. In fact, you are the only one to know of it.
I did not think he wanted it bruited about to those
in his mourning lines, for though he may have left
the sea to seek someone, he found me instead. I let
our relationship stand as the marker for his immortality.

When Mar-keshan took Gray's hand they ex-
changed looks and names. She called him Mar from
then on, meaning simply "Man from Waters." He
was the only one in L'Lal'dome to call her Linni.

They disappeared at once into the inner rooms where the servants live. If I had thought that after a bath she would emerge already transformed in the silken gowns of court, I was sadly mistaken. Mar-keshan swore to me that he had laid out a magnificent swath of silk for her, but she presented herself to me, with a slight bob of her head, in the same gray gown. Its wrinkles had been steamed out by Mar-keshan's attentions, but it was no more flattering than before. She had plaited her hair, though, and with Mar-keshan's help had fashioned it back up in a crown twined with some of the colorful flowers plucked from the courtyard gardens: golden-eyed Wood-cheese, trailing Mourning Glory, and a spray of Queen's Breath all purple and pink.

"Am I . . . presentable?" she asked. She did not ask if she looked well, if she were pretty, or some other coquetry. Simply *presentable*.

I would not lie to her.

"Presentable," I said.

Mar-keshan grunted and she turned to him.

"If you stand tall, they will know your true beauty," he said. "Beauty is in the bearing."

She smiled at him. "You sound like my mother."

"And her grandmother," I added.

She looked at me and perhaps my tone had been ungentle, but she did not comment further. So once again in silence we went out through the winding halls.

Tell me about those halls. I never could map them.

The princes' apartments in L'Lal'dome are in an ever-spiraling circle like the whorls of shells that sometimes wash up onto our shore. Why should you try to make a map of them?

So that I might find my way alone.

Only a prince may walk those halls. Only a prince and those who companion or serve him.

Call it—curiosity, then.

You sky-farers have a strange curiosity. It drives you ever outward. Does it drive you inward as well?

What we learn of the outward world we apply to the inward.

Then think of a shell. Like a true man of Waters, Mar-keshan collected such shells and he once gave me a prize one, whole and unmarked, sliced through and both halves mounted on a wooden stand. We have a musical term for such a pattern as well. We call it lara'lani, a circle-puzzle.

We have such things on our home world as well. They are called chambered nautilus.

Cham'bured naut'lus. A strange word.

The word chamber *also means living space or apartment.*

How fine. I love playing with words. But you see, we needed no maps. The apartments, the cham'burs, were not mazes to a prince. Of all the places in our world it is what I know the best. But for the uninitiated, the place is truly a circle-puzzle, a labyrinth. I expected therefore to see puzzlement writ large on Gray's face.

But she followed me with that same silent grace, head high, not a word about the spiraled puzzle path we traced.

In the very center of the lara'lani lived the Queen, though there is more than one entrance to those apartments. Still, when coming for an audience, it is the main spiral that one always uses for approach. At each footfall, once past the Apartments of Princes, bells announce the way. I used those bells thematically in the second section of my song cycle, repeating them near the end of the songs, a refrain and a death knell at once.

I remember it well. I thought the bells beautifully punctuated the phrasing.

Punctuation? Yes. Exactly. How clever of you. . . . But of course. You are a musician, too.

Only the bells seemed to bring Gray out of her silence. She said, "I am called—" then stopped.

I shrugged. One can get used to any cacophony, make music out of the strangest sounds.

She shook her head as if shaking the thoughts free. Just as she did, the great wooden doors opened.

Heads turned toward us. I saw T'arremos, smirking, hiding his map-face behind a ringed hand. And my brother princes, those who had already completed their missions, in the bright colors of the Queen's Consort, turned on their cushions and looked up as we walked in.

On the first and second levels below the Queen's dais, on twenty cushions each, lay C'arrademos and D'oremos, their faces showing no more emotion than the stone caryatids outside. On the highest level, surrounded by the thirty cushions of Queenship, lay the Queen herself. Long and slim, so slim the skin seemed neatly tailored over her bones, she made no move except a blink. So Royalty schools itself.

We waited for a signal from her. At last she moved her hand. I pulled Gray to my side, then with a little nudge started her down the aisle and followed close behind.

Without looking back at me to make sure she was doing the right thing—which any other girl from

Lands might have done—Gray walked to the foot of the risers. C'arrademos tucked his feet under his buttocks to make room for her to walk up, but D'oremos did not move.

"Come, child," said the Queen, leaning forward and holding out her hand, a singular honor indeed.

Gray walked up the stairs. By accident she stepped on a corner of C'arrademos's outermost cushion, which caused great consternation in the Hall; but Gray did not falter. She stepped over D'oremos, which saved him from a like humiliation. And when she was on the level with the Queen, she knelt and took the Queen's proferred hand.

I closed my eyes. I think I moaned aloud, waiting for some awful blow to fall. One simply does not *touch* the Queen in public unless she demands it with the proper words and signs. And then into the silence I heard Gray's voice, though it could not have gone farther than where I stood. I do not think she meant her words to go even that far, for I had to strain to hear them. What she said was meant only for the Queen.

"Do not fear the dark, my lady, for I am sent to light your way."

It was the simplest of speeches, the language straight out of the Middle Lands. Later on, of course, she was to learn the more ornate court speech, but she never used it in her poems. There were Royals who criticized her for it, but she was right to hold to her own.

The Queen patted one of the lesser cushions by her side and bade Gray sit. Without hesitation or a formal demur, she sat.

It made the greatest sensation the court had ever seen. C'arrademos bit his lip. D'oremos turned to wink at me and I knelt at the bottom of the stairs until the servants brought me my ten pillows. When I sank back against them I realized I was weak and shaking and, strange to say, there were tears in my eyes.

The Queen used her court voice, which seemed quiet but could carry to the very walls and beyond. It is a trick of Queens to speak so. Even as a King for almost a year I have yet to master that voice, and *I* was trained as a singer.

"Let me see your poems, child, the ones I have been told about."

If Gray had been one of us, a prince or other Royal, there would have followed an elaborate show of apology or regret, cozening and coyness, then final reluctant obedience. But Gray knew none of the games of court. She reached into her small reed basket immediately and drew out a handful of poems.

"Read them to me, child," said the Queen in her inimitable voice. She lay back against the cushions and closed her eyes.

Gray began to read, starting with the original Gray Wanderer poem, whispering it to the Queen.

"Louder," instructed the Queen, "that we may *all* hear them."

For the first time Gray looked unsure. There were some thirty princes in the room, and though they had eager attentiveness written on their faces, there was a kind of predatory quality to the look. Gray whispered something to the Queen and she smiled.

"B'oremos," said the Queen.

I sat up, still shaking.

"Go to your room at once and bring your plecta
and sing me the song that you wrote to accompany
this poem. We will wait."

I hurried from the room, face flushed but trium-
phant. I did not even glance at T'arremos, though
I could just imagine the blue veins running through
the map on his cheek like pulsing, angry rivers to
the sea.

Mar-keshan was standing at the doorway of my
apartment with the plecta in hand. How he knew
what I wanted was one of those many small mys-
teries of the servant class. I was just grateful that
he served so well. I grabbed the instrument from
him and, tuning as I went, hurried back along the
whorls of the halls, past the bells, to the Queen's
Public Room.

It was as if no one had moved since I left. Along
the aisle leading to the risers were the princes on
their cushions, with T'arremos on his knees still
aghast at my good fortune. The Queen was leaning
back, eyes closed. Her two advisers on the second
and third levels were wide-eyed and waiting. Hands
folded, Gray sat as if the silence in the room had
given her permission to think.

When I reached the bottom of the levels, I
strummed a full chord on the plecta. Its voice was
strong and echoed beautifully with the harmonics
that bounded off the rounded walls.

I sang, slowly at first, then with gathering
strength. And when I was done, Gray began to recite
five other poems. They were good, solid accom-
paniments to the first, a strong beginning to the Gray
Wanderer Cycle, though the third one, which begins
"What isles are we . . ." is rarely heard anymore.
It was hard to believe that a girl of Lands just out

of the blush of childhood could have written them.
The last was her very famous "Valediction."

The Queen sighed and waved her hand in a complicated pattern that was the signal for the priestesses to come forth.

A door slid open to the left of the cushions and
three members of Moons stepped out.

What vestments were they wearing?

The belted white kirtles for prophesying and the
diadems, with the moon phases, on their shaven
heads. The eldest priestess was the seer, though
sometimes it is a younger one who has the gift of
seeing time. She carried the rood of augury in one
hand, the orb of prophecy in the other. Only when
she had bowed to the Queen did she hand over the
precious relicts to her acolytes.

The Queen nodded to them. "What do you know
of a child of Lands?" asked the Queen.

The old priestess looked into the orb that one
acolyte held cradled in her palms. For a moment the
orb seemed to emit a blue light. I was awed at the
time, but I have since been told by a sky-farer the
secret of that inner flame. There is a cache of oil
inside the globe and a pair of flints that strike when
a certain mechanism is touched.

*Whoever told you was wrong to do so. It is our
vow to observe, to study, to learn.*

As King it is my duty to know everything. Besides, the young man was drunk on royal wine at
the time. It is better that I know the secret of the
Moons' magic. Believe me, I have told no one.

You have told me.

You will not let it go further. You dare not, if
you have learned our customs well.

What did the priestess say?

"A child of Lands shall lead the way," was what she said.

The aisle princes oohed at this revelation. I kept silent and looked at Gray. Her head was bowed but her face was composed.

"And is *this* the child?" asked the Queen. One may ask a single question more of prophesy.

The priestess turned and grasped the rood where the two sticks cross, two fingers on either side of the upright stand and her thumb across the middle.

"She shall be betrayed but she shall remain true."

The Queen dismissed them. It is said that the prophesies of Moons are always accurate but that one never understands them until long afterward.

"So you shall remain true to me," the Queen said to Gray, choosing to ignore the rest of the augury. "That is, if you are really the child of Lands of whom we have been told. Come, show me you are indeed that child."

"And how may I do that, my lady?" Gray asked, looking directly at the Queen.

"By composing another threnody now, while I watch. How do I know you did not simply borrow your poems from the promptings of your elders?"

Gray looked down at D'oremos and he stirred uneasily as if sensing what was to come.

"But I have no one to grieve for, my Queen," Gray said.

The Queen smiled. "Nor have I," she said. "But time delivers us all to grief. Let us eat now and talk no more of dying." Her hand signaled the servants and the Hall was turned at once into a feast place. I got to play dances instead of dirges and the resultant melodies made even Gray smile.

• • •

It was past the peak of night when we were dismissed at last from the Queen's Public Room and Gray was beyond exhaustion. The flowers twined in her hair had long since wilted. Her gray gown was wrinkled and stained past—I would guess— even Mar-keshan's abilities to reclaim it. There were faint red lines traveling like rivulets to the golden centers of her eyes. Of course I, used to court nights, was not as tired, but I faked weariness and sent her along to her bed.

Before disappearing, she turned in the doorway. "For all that you have done . . ." she began.

I turned away quickly. I did not want thanks or pity or whatever else I read in those tired eyes. In fact, I was no longer sure *what* I wanted of her.

She took the dismissal as her due. Lands girls are always so sentimental. I listened as her footsteps faded away.

Then I hung the plecta on the wall and the last resonances of its strings died away as well. That sigh of the instrument on the wall always moves me enormously. I blinked back a tear and turned.

There was a messenger bowed down on the rug by my outer door.

"Prince B'oremos," he whispered.

I knew from his rainbow loincloth that he came from the Queen.

"Speak."

"She summons you."

I guess I was not entirely surprised, but still I could feel my stomach tighten, my organs engorge with a rush of blood. It was the first call I had had. . . . I looked quickly down the lean line of my body.

"I am ready," I said and followed him out
through the halls.

We did not go along the main public way but
along the Pleasure Path to the Queen's secret back
door. The walls were muraled with scenes of tumbling, of naked male with naked male or female,
though of course there was no picture of a naked
Queen.

The servant did not enter the Pleasure Door, but
I knew it at once. How often had we whispered
about that famous portal, with the words of the Prin-
ciple carved into the lintel: *Burn the fierce light of
pleasure before the dark cave*. And I wondered, as
generations of princes before me, how it would feel
to sow the Queen, to have her long, slim legs around
me and to run my fingers through the dark ropes of
her hair. Surely it would be different from the
sweaty couplings with plump Lands girls or with an
occasional scale-skinned girl from Waters. Queens
do not sweat.

The lamps were low, their small flames made gen-
tler by the colored glass that framed them: oranges
and blues and a filtered green that reminded me of
the sea off the shore of L'Lal'dome. Shadows
played across the ceiling where silken hangings blew
and billowed in the pulsing air.

The Queen lay back against her cushions, a
darker shadow than the ones dancing above her. She
did not move, not even to wave a hand to call me
in. I could not see her mouth but she spoke to me
in that court whisper. I thought, flushing, pleased,
that every room in L'Lal'dome must have echoed
with her royal command.

"Come, B'oremos, plow me. Give me a girl child
that my line may live."

And I tried. Oh, how I tried. All the positions and words and gyrations I had practiced and had been taught in my foreshortened mission year I applied to the Queen's unresponding body. All the while she breathed shallowly in my ear. I never raised her to a moment of passion.

And when I was done, having spent my coin three times in her purse, she lay as unmoving as at the first.

"Well plowed," she said, speaking the ritual words to me. There was not even a change in her voice, not a bit of rushed breath or fading delight. Then she added in an undertone that I had to bend over her to hear. "Your enthusiasm and loyalty are to be commended."

"My Queen," I answered in exhaustion.

"And now," she whispered, rising up slowly onto one elbow, "I have a task for you for which you have just received first payment."

"My lady," I said.

She told me. It was to be the first betrayal.

Tape 6:

THE SEVEN GRIEVERS, PART III

Place: _Queen's Hall of Grief, Room of Instruction_

Time: _Queen's Time 23, Thirteenth Matriarchy;
labtime 2132.5 +_ A.D.

Speaker: _Queen's Own Griever to the apprentices,
including Lina-Lania_

Permission: _No permission, preset, voice-
activated_

And here ends the song of the Seven Grievers as
was told Master to Master down through the lines
from the hour of the sisters' joining to the moment
of my tongue's speaking. I have saved these woeful
songs in my mouth and in my heart for the time
when, as the Queen's Own Griever, I may have to
wail for the dying of the land once again.

Hear, then, and listen well. My word is firm,
firmer than sleep or the Cup that carries it, firmer
than the strength of heroes. My voice makes the
telling true. To listen, to remember, is to know.

So the Night-Seers became the walkers in the
day, six great families: Lands, Moons, Stars,
Rocks, Waters, and Arcs and Bow. And they were
dark and dark-seeing still; few indeed were their
smiles.

But of the People of L'Lal'ladia, the Place of
Blessing and Rejoicing, there remained but two who
were not drowned. Two there were who had hidden
themselves from the rising waters, a brother and a

sister who had bound themselves in an empty cask and floated out upon the very face of the sea.

For the one hundred times one hundred days and nights, the two lay entwined in the wooden womb, rocked by the waters. And the only sound they heard was the lapping of the waves upon their boat.

But then they thought they heard another sound, the dolorous chants of their dark sisters weeping upon a new-made shore. So the brother and sister untwined themselves and pushed up the cover of their cask and revealed themselves to the watchers on the shore.

And when they were hauled in by the nets of Waters and set upon the land, the Night-Seers saw that these two were unlike themselves, being tall and slim and fair.

"Come," said the two, "there is still song in the world other than dirges. There is still light that pierces the night. We who are taller than you, we can see farther. We who are slimmer than you, we can run faster. We who are fairer-skinned than you, we are closer to the Light."

And the darker children saw this was so and knelt before the two.

"We will make a place of beauty, a place of feasting and rejoicing. And you shall come to us and serve us."

And the six grieving families saw that it was so.

Then the tall sister said, "Because it is not right that my brother alone, who is all but past the time of seeding, shall plow me, you shall send your tallest sons to me to do their duty. And in turn I shall send my sons to your daughters. But the tallest and fairest shall dwell with me in the place of beauty."

And it was so.

So the six dark grievers serve the seventh, drinking from them the sweet milk of blessing and rejoicing. And the seventh family was known as Royals. It was their duty to shine brightly and rule lightly and recall by their presence the blessing and rejoicing of L'Lal'ladia in the long and dolorous dark days of L'Lal'lor.

Selah.

Tape 7:

BETRAYALS

Place: *Palace of the King, Apartment of the King*
Time: *King's Time 1, First Patriarchy; 2137.5 +*
A.D.
Speaker: *the King, called B'oremos, also called*
the Singer of Dirges, to anthropologist
Aaron Spenser
Permission: *King's own*

Traitor is such a soft word, don't you think? And
what, after all, is a betrayal? What I did *to* Gray, I
did *for* her as well. She became stronger, she grew
in her art because of it. And besides, I was only
following the Queen's orders. So where was the betrayal? Whom did I really betray?

I rode off that very night, my skin still smelling
from the Queen's unguents and scents. She lent me
a mount from her own stable, a perfumed white
charger that lifted its feet clumsily along the cob-
blestones but once in the meadows was swift as ar-
rowshot.

In the fields I could see last year's liliroot nodding
in the passing winds. Purple-and-white sweet lanni
and wild narsis covered the hillocks. And along the
ridges, capped with windstrife, were clouds like
gray puddles against the darker sky. Nightsight, we
say, is truesight. It is the one gift of the Common
Grievers we have bred into Royal lines.

As I rode, it was as if I saw everything anew, as
if I had been born again to represent all the lost
celebrations of our kind. It is said that the Queen's
first touch renews the spirit. For me that was cer-

tainly true. I rode toward the complacent Middle
Lands with an enthusiasm I had not felt my entire
mission year. I even hummed as I rode, the horse's
gait lending a strange vibrato to my voice.

It took me a day and a night more to reach the
millhouse where Gray's mother and grandmother
ruled over that houseful of slack-jawed, runny-
nosed boys.

If my coming surprised them, they let me in without too many questions and only a single argument
between them. I assured them that their Linni was
comfortable and had already made a great impression at court. Three times I had to tell them of her
entrance down the aisle of princes: how she looked,
what she wore, who had dressed her hair. I told
them what the Queen had said and what Linni had
said in return, but I did not mention the priestess's
words. I did not mention *betrayal*. If they sensed it
behind my stories, they did not say.

At last we sat down for dinner, the usual over-
cooked and understrained common meal of Lands.
The greens were limp and the meat—some kind of
local fowl—had been boiled until its wings had
fallen off. I pushed it around my plate enough times
to seem interested.

The three brothers had questions about the white
charger, for they had unsaddled it and stabled it
willingly.

"Is it fast?" asked the youngest.

"Faster than the wind," I assured him, which
said little since the winds across Lands are soft and
slow.

"Does it handle easily?" asked the eldest.

"*It* is a *she*, and the handling is all done with
wrists and thighs," I explained, showing them and

thus ending my charade with the tasteless meal. They aped my gestures until, at a signal from their grandmother, the youngest rose to clear the table.

I let them finger the leather leggings I wore over my rainbow-colored kirtle. The padding on the inside of the thighs made them giggle until I pointed out how chafed a rider might become without such extra padding. "Though," I added, "no one but a true Royal needs extra padding." A lesson at such a time is always a good idea with these doltish Lands boys.

Their mother smiled and nodded at my bit of moralizing, though her mother frowned.

"Linni could use it," said the younger boy, coming back with a damp cloth to make a swipe at the table, clearing it of the few crumbs. There was a scramble at our feet as the house pets fought over the scraps.

"Stick legs. Old bony behind and fore." It was the middle boy, the one from the Hall. He and his sister had obviously never been close, though for him to speak so in front of me meant the name-calling was more ritual than real.

I cuffed him anyway, before his mother could speak to him. He looked at me through slotted eyes but made no sound, not even a whimper. "She is a Royal now, your sister, your better. You will not use such words about her again." There was no arguing with my tone and he knew it.

Rising, I said, "I would sleep here tonight and tomorrow have a quiet word with Granny alone."

There was a sudden small silence in the room; it chilled me even though the fire in the hearth chose that moment to flare into life, a small pocket of sap

bursting in a piece of wood. Then the two women
spoke at once.

"It will be so," said the granny.

"I will make your bed up," said the mother.

I took the slack-jawed middle boy to bed with
me, more for punishment than amusement. I wanted
to hurt him again for his name-calling and I was not
gentle with him. He did not complain of it, indeed
he did not have enough imagination or experience
to do that. But even his presence in the bed did not
warm me. I spent most of the night awake, trying
to imagine in what way he and Gray were related.
Only at the end did I realize that it was to the Lands
girl Linni he was linked, not the Royal Gray. The
Gray Wanderer was someone he would know only
in story and in song. A strange sowing that must
have been, so many years before, that had deposited
that particular nestling in this particular nest.

Morning finally arrived and when I arose and
parted the curtains there was no one left at home
but the grandmother and me. The boys had all fled
to their chores and their mother was at the Hall
tidying the memoria for another day of grieving.

"Old woman," I said.

She turned toward me, her face unreadable, and
smoothed her hands down the sides of her worn gray
skirts.

"She will be a great griever," I said. "Perhaps
the greatest our world has ever known."

She nodded.

"And the Queen would have her begin now,
crafting poems of grief. But . . ."

She nodded again. It was then that I saw the intelligence shining in her eyes and it became clear to

me that Gray had sprung from a line of crafty Lands
women, though the planting was of a Royal seed. I
really needed to go no further, but truth impelled
me. "The Queen has sent me to—"

She cut me short. "You will make them remember me?" she asked, her eyes suddenly luminous,
her mouth opening wide.

"Grandmother, I will."

"Then I will make up the attic room. It has not
been given a shaking since the departure of our
Grieven One." She turned and left me to stare into
the fire. I heard her footsteps going up the wooden
treads and the creaking of the floorboards overhead.
The morning fire was only bright embers, but the
embers seemed haloed with rainbows. I held my
hands out to the hearth but I felt no warmth.

I do not know how long I stared at the dying fire,
but there was a sudden touch at my elbow. I jerked
around. It was the old woman. She held out a Cup
to me. Clearly it was a family treasure, cut from a
single piece of black stone and expertly faceted,
centuries old. I took it and it was a solid, balanced
weight between my hands. I could feel the carvings
imprinting on my palms as I rolled it between them.

"I will change now," she said.

"I will fill the Cup," I answered.

I sat for a long moment at the table before I
began, thinking about Gray and how she had looked
at me, her face calm, whispering, "For all that you
have done . . ." Have done! All that I was now
doing was for her, too, though it was the Queen who
required it. Then the face of the Queen, avid, vul-
pine, full of eager plottings, replaced Gray's in my
mind.

I took a small silk purse from around my neck,
and opened it, and was assailed at once by a vivid
musky odor. I tipped the purse and three dark kernels of Lumin fell out.

Only the Queen uses the Lumin nut. One small
kernel can cause nights of sensual phantoms and
phantasmagoria. Two can provoke hysteria and
nightmare. Three kernels, soaked in wine, lead to
a short, dream-filled sleep and death. It is the quickest, most painless death we can give. That is why
only the Queen is allowed the use of the kernels.
There are two Lumin trees that grow in her courtyard. All others, save for some that may be in the
deepest, most impenetrable part of the forest, have
been destroyed.

I looked at the kernels and sighed. Someone like
T'arremos might have been tempted to pocket the
nuts and smother the old woman instead. But I had
had my orders and, besides, she was Gray's grandmother. She would not suffer at my hands.

I picked up the kernels and dropped them one by
one into the Cup. The faintest *tink* was all I heard.
Then I poured a bit of Queen's wine from a flask I
had carried with me. It would not do to send the
old woman on her final journey with that common
Lands swill. She would go in style; that was my very
own idea.

"I am ready," she said.

I turned to look at her. She was standing by the
stairway dressed in a long dark gown that covered
her from neck to ankles. Lands go covered to their
deaths while we Royals are laid out with only a dia-
phanous silken sheet over us. I did not show any
emotion, even by a blink, for I did not want to shame
her.

I followed her silently up the stairs, or at least as silently as the stairs allowed, for they sighed and moaned under our combined weight, a curious accompaniment to the journey.

The upstairs room was windowless, the thatch old, and there was a distinctive smell of mold about. The darkness was illumined by a single candle and in that small light I could clearly see the bed, its posters ornately carved, the linen sparkling clean. A drawing of rood and orb hung over the bed.

Without any extra fuss, the old woman lay down and put her hands one atop another over her stomach. "I need not confess to you," she said. "I spoke my final piece to my daughter last night."

I nodded. They had both known. These Lands women breed true. Gray's lines were firm.

I knelt down beside her and held out the Cup. "Come, take the Cup," I said. "You will like the wine. It comes"—I hesitated, then chose the lic— "with the Queen's blessing and with three kernels from her Lumin trees."

She took the Cup without a moment's hesitation and drained it as if eager for sleep. Then she handed it back.

As the drugged wine took effect, her eyes grew first bright, then fogged. Her mouth began to stretch in that rictus we call the Smile of the Dead. She whispered and the snatches I heard convinced me that her dreams had started, for she spoke of bright and holy things.

I began to rise and her hand shot out and held my arm. She half rose onto one elbow. "You will make them remember me?"

"I will."

"May your lines of grieving be long," she said, her voice graveled and slow. She lay back and closed her eyes.

"May your time of dying be short," I answered and sank down by her side again. I stayed there until she stopped breathing. Then I put two funerary gems on her eyelids, another gift from the Queen, and left.

I had planned to stop only briefly at the Hall of Grief, long enough to tell Gray's mother about her mother's death, touch the boys, and be gone. But when Gray's mother saw me, her eyes met mine for a minute, then slid away as if she did not want to know the truth. She brought the back of her hand to her mouth. I wondered that she was so moved; she had always been fighting with the old woman.

Then she turned and whispered something to the older and younger of the boys. They left the Hall at once, to go home to put their grandmother's husk out.

I knew then I had to honor the old woman's dying request. I stepped to Gray's mother's side. "Granny's time of dying was short," I said.

She nodded, still not looking at me.

"I would grieve for her," I said.

Still she seemed not to understand.

"I would remain for the Seven and grieve for her," I said. "I do it waiving payment, and for the respect I feel."

Mutely she accepted.

"Send this boy"—I fingered his shoulder hard— "to L'Lal'dome to tell Gray . . . Linni . . . that her grandmother is dead. Tell her that there was no pain, that there were bright dreams and an easy sleep in the end. Tell her . . . that I grieve with her.''

The boy left at once. I lent him the white horse and I understand he rode it as if born to the saddle. I had not expected that. Rather, I thought he would fall often and probably lose the horse, and have to limp into the city to deliver his message. But he clung to the saddle like a bellywort burr. It was his single talent.

I do not think Gray's mother spoke to me the entire time. Without her own mother to argue with, she seemed tongueless. But I called many mourners to the old woman's lines; she was well and truly grieved. I think her daughter had some satisfaction in that.

By the end of the Seven the boy had returned with the horse and I rode it home. He did not talk of the great city; I did not ask. But I saw the longing for it in his eyes. He would be jealous of his sister from now on. She would be Stick-legs to him no more.

All of L'Lal'dome was abuzz with Gray's grieving when I arrived. She had written lyric after lyric, a wild flowering of grief. But if I thought to profit from her fame or get to touch her, I was wrong. Immediately after the Seven, she had been apprenticed to the Master Griever, the Queen's Own, and no one but the Master and the Queen herself would be allowed to talk to her for that training year.

Then what happened in that year?

She lived and ate and slept in the House of Instruction, the small house that is in the inner courtyard of the Queen's Apartments. That much I know. But the Master Grievers guard their secrets well. We are told only that the apprentices must learn the prime tales and the subsidiary tales as well. They must hold all the learning of the land comfortably in their mouths. There are three steps: Purity of Mouth, Purity of Mind, Purity of Heart. But of these, I know only the names and not what they mean.

But you are the King.

But I am not the Queen. And I am not a Master Griever.

I saw Gray twice on the walkways and once in the Queen's Hall of Grief when she helped prepare the table for the mourning of the Queen's last living sister. But I was not allowed to speak to her, for she was at that moment being purified of all but the tales she had to learn. They call it "being reborn." She was being reborn into a Master Griever.

Becoming a Master Griever is a process that usually takes half a lifetime, there is so much to learn, but Gray accomplished it in a year. And it may be that is why what happened happened. She was still so young, too young, perhaps. But who was to know then? Had not the priestess prophesied, "A child of Lands shall lead the way"? We all believed that Gray was that child.

Beware of prophesy.

I went to Gray's confirmation. Indeed, the entire court was there. Even the mission princes had been recalled, something that had never been done before.

We stood by our cushions as Gray was marched down between the aisles, flanked by D'oremos on her right and C'arrademos on her left. Her hair was loose within a net of tiny glittering gems. She was covered head to toe in a white linen cape, and as she walked to the foot of the Queen's riser, she seemed encapsulated in silence.

When the three of them reached the riser, the two princes knelt by her side and each held on to the hem of her garment. Giving simultaneous tugs, they freed the cape from her shoulders, and it fell to the ground. She stood clothed in a slate-gray silk with a belting of precious stones that left her arms bare to the shoulders.

The priestesses came out of the door to the left of the cushions. The seer took the rood, touching it to Gray's mouth, her forehead, then, slipping the gown down and baring Gray's small left breast, she touched the rood to the place over the heart.

Gray did not move, even when the priestess had gone back to her place by the door.

Then the Queen rose from her cushions and walked down the stairs until she was face-to-face with Gray. With tenderness, she covered Gray's left breast again with the silk. Then she suddenly kissed Gray full on the mouth.

Taking a step back, she said, "I give you breath, sister. Give me immortality."

And thus was Gray, who was no blood tie to the Queen, made the Queen's Own Griever.

There was no small consternation in this act as the Queen's Own Griever, an ancient cousin several times removed, still lived. But she left the room at once and was found hours later, lying on her eighteen cushions, under her silken death sheet, eyes open and staring but quite, quite dead.

It has since been said that the priestess prophesied the old Griever's death at the service and that is why the Queen had given Gray the kiss of kinship. But I was there and standing close to the front. Be-

lieve me, the priestess said nothing. And Gray, I am
certain, had been shocked at the time, her eyes flick-
ing open at the kiss, her grief at her beloved teach-
er's death very real. She mourned the old lady twice
the Seven, an excess of grief, until the Queen herself
commanded that she stop and that she forget what
had happened. She stopped, and perhaps she forgot,
for Gray was a great believer in the Queen's Truth,
but it was as if some light in her eyes had been
shuttered. Her poems for that particular death were
full of the images of bleeding wounds. Those poems
have never, to my knowledge, been recorded.

You remember so much.

I certainly remember that, sky-farer, for it was
the first time Gray came to me.

Came to you?

To be caressed, though I was not expecting it.
The Queen's Own Griever is an Untouchable. Her
vows are ones of celibacy and tears. I had been
mourning all one evening, less for the old Griever
than for my lost chances with Gray, flinging myself
angrily at my pillows. And when called to the
Queen—who was always insatiable through periods
of grief—I performed the rites of sowing with such
thrusts and groaning, I all but damaged us both, to
her pleasure and my everlasting shame. So I was
there with the Queen a long time, for though other
princes had been called upon earlier, I was that
year's favorite and I had been called upon the most.
I went each night, sometimes twice a night, returning to my rooms exhausted but unrelieved, covered
with my own perspiration and the Queen's scent.
Queens, as I have said, do not sweat but their touch
leaves a man smelling in a way that baths do not
quickly erase.

It was the tenth day after the death of the old Master, and when I came into my apartment, Gray was pacing in front of the wall of viols. Mar-keshan was pleading with her to leave. They were so engrossed with their argument they did not hear me enter.

"He may be hours getting back," Mar-keshan said. "The Queen keeps him until she tires him or tires of him, whichever comes first."

"I must speak to him," Gray insisted. "Mar, please. I *must*."

"He is not here."

"I am here."

They turned to me at the same time and, with a small cry like that of a wounded creature, Gray ran to me and threw herself into my arms.

Mar-keshan bowed quickly and left before I had a chance to read his face.

I put my hands on either side of Gray's head and turned her face up to me. "I am here," I said again, this time as softly as a touch.

And . . .

And that was it. We sat together and talked all night. I was too tired for anything else and she had her vows, after all. Often we lay back on my cushions and my fingers gently outlined her face, her lips, as she spoke, but otherwise . . .

I knew that.

You guessed that.

As you will.

She came to me another time. Long after.

Long after?

Long after I had betrayed her a second and yet a third time. Long after my five years of sowing were done and I could not have sown her even if I had desired it. We lay together all night in one an-

other's arms, for it was the night that Mar-keshan
died. And it mattered not between friends, then, that
in the past there had been betrayals.

You said there was really no betrayal.

And what a King says is true. But there was—
and there was not—betrayal. Let me tell you of the
second and you may judge for yourself.

.   It was a season later that the first of your sky-
ships came down. It landed, as you know, just outside L'Lal'dome. The priestess went with rood and
orb, surrounded by her archers, and proclaimed that
this was as the old prophesy foretold.

The Queen, who watched from the Jutting tower,
sent word: "Which prophesy?"

And the answer came back, "The one made in
the Tenth Matriarchy which said that *the sky will
open and spit forth a wonder.*"

The Queen spoke with C'arrademos, who remembered vaguely such a warning. D'oremos reminded them both that the prophesy had been ful-
filled in the Twelfth Matriarchy when there had been
a brief rain of hard stones. The Queen then thought
about both these things and went down the tower
and onto the plain herself.

Behind her traipsed a handful of the young
princes. I was by her side, being the current favorite. She pushed through the archers and then she
and I—the other princes remaining prudently behind the company of Arcs and Bow—stood face-to-
face with the priestess.

"What do you read in the orb, sister?" the Queen
asked.

The priestess shook her head. "The Light has
failed, my Queen. There is nothing to be read there;

the shadow of this great moving tower puts out the small light of the orb.''

The Queen looked at the orb and saw it was true.

"Let me go and call out what dwells within this thing," I said, thinking that if I died for the Queen I would at least have Gray to grieve for me.

"Go," she said, a bit more quickly than I had expected.

I turned and looked at the other princes, and T'arremos smirked openly. So I squared my shoulders and walked over to the great silver tower and rang my knuckles against its side. It echoed strangely, a hollow sound that told me it was not solid throughout. And then a door on the side opened and a silver stair unfolded, after which the first of you sky-farers came down.

I will tell you how he looked to us: tall, unflinching, with that great globe upon his head which was subsequently discarded but which at first we thought *was* his head. We marveled at his silver garment that did not shift or change in the wind.

Then he took off the helm, which had showed us only reflections of ourselves, to display a face that seemed almost a parody of our own. He held up his hand in a sign we later understood meant peace. Then he smiled, a grimace as broad as any dying man's.

"I am not an enemy," he said, his voice thick around our words, but still understandable.

"Why should you be?" asked the Queen.

Then the ship disgorged seven more just like the first and the last one was you, Man Without Tears.

How did I look to you?

As you do now, A'ron. Oh, your hair is longer, but it is still that same gold, the color of a meadow flower, of the Queen's eyes, of the sun. We all mar-

velled at that. And though you now cover your face
with a beard as golden as your head of hair, the
broad planes of the face under it are the same. And
the green of your eyes. Though it is fifty years since
last we met, you look the same.

The years sit well on you, too, B'oremos.

That is yet another prerogative of Royals. We do
not age as the Common Grievers do. You do not
age, either.

*I age normally. But my time—up there—is dif-
ferent.*

So we have surmised. But then we have had a
long time for making guesses and wondering.

Are we sky-farers, then, still a wonder to you?

You are something to wonder at. But the six
Common Grievers came from caves and we Royals
from a cask in the sea. Why should there not be a
people come down from the sky?

Are you afraid of us?

I was a little, at first. And then I was not. And
then it was too late to be afraid. In a time of changes,
one does not fear a little change. One fears the end
of all changes.

*Then, if you are not afraid of me, tell me about
that second betrayal.*

The second betrayal had to do with you, A'ron.
And Gray long since forgave me. I wonder if you
will do the same.

Do I know what it is?

I think you do.

*Then I have already forgiven you. If I know it
not, then it was not important enough to forgive.*

You knew—and you did not know. Search your
own story, A'ron, for the betrayal is there.

Tape 8:

THE MAN WITHOUT TEARS

Place: *Space Lab Common Room*
Time: *2132.9 A.D.*
Speaker: *Captain James Macdonald of USS Venture; Lieutenant Debra Malkin; various other unidentified officers; Aaron Spenser, B.S., M.S., Ph.D., Star Certificate 987643368OK*
Permission: *Captain's log, mandated USS Code #09863*

This inquiry into the actions of Aaron Spenser, Anthropologist First Class re Mission Henderson's IV is declared open on A.D. 9/11/2132, at 1100 hours. The charge is Cultural Contamination as defined by the USS Code #27. The specification is that you, Aaron Spenser, did willfully and unlawfully violate the Cultural Contact Contamination Act in regards to your relationship with an inhabitant or inhabitants of the newly opened planet Henderson's IV in such a way that you have influenced—to the good or to the bad—all culture within their closed system forever. How say you to the specification, guilty or not guilty?

I have been more changed than they by the contact, Lieutenant Malkin.

Guilty or not guilty to the specification?

Guilty—*and* not guilty, Lieutenant.

How say you to the charge?

Guilty—I guess. But Captain, ladies and gentlemen, it is not that cut and dried, if you'll forgive me. There were circumstances—

How say you to the charge, Anthro Spenser?
Guilty or not guilty?

I can't answer that easily.

You must answer. Guilty or not guilty?

Just a minute, Lieutenant, I think we can handle this a bit less rigidly.

But the rules of Court Martial, sir.

This is my ship, Lieutenant, and we can make anything that does not conform strictly to the rules off the record later, if necessary.

Yes, sir.

Now, Aaron, you have been shipboard for almost three years, counting travel time, and we've gotten to know one another pretty well.

Yes, sir.

And in preparation for this empanelment, I even read your early papers on Egyptians with the wonderful tag from that poet. What was his name?

Carew, sir. A favorite of mine.

Ah, yes, Carew. Well, I'm not much for poetry myself, though I do have a fondness for another early Earth rhymer. His name was Nash.

Not exactly the same century, sir.

No? Well it doesn't matter.

I appreciate your trying to put me at my case, sir. But what might be best is if I just simply tell the story from beginning to end: about what happened to Linni and me.

Linni?

Linni. The one they call the Gray Wanderer.

That's the formidable tall girl, right?

Tall, yes, sir. Though not really so tall. I'm taller by a couple of inches, and I'm six two. And not so formidable. Vulnerable, really. Lonely. Hurt or wounded. Shy. And young.

You're not so old yourself, son.

No, sir. I'm twenty-two, sir.

Sir, I really must protest. The Court Martial—

Lieutenant, if you would just listen, you would hear. We have already begun the Court Martial inquiry. Carry on, Aaron.

Yes, sir.

It started before we touched down. We had to learn about them as best we could before actually greeting them. We had to minimize culture shock—on their part but also, I think, on ours. What we learned, after breaking down their language, which is liquid and full of bubbling sighs and soft glottals—not unlike Earth Polynesian—is that in their folklore they referred to themselves and their world as the Land of the Grievers or the Place of Grieving. For us, though we learned about it early, it became the hardest concept to grasp, for we come from a culture that tries to push grief into the background of our lives, bury it. I was reminded, as I studied the tapes, of a tombstone next to my mother's. She was buried in a small old country cemetery in Vermont—that's Earth, sir—where she had lived all of her life. Where I have lived all of mine until she died and I was sent to stay with my father near the spaceport in Florida. The tombstone had been barely readable, but I'd been able to make it out. "It is a fearful thing to love what death can touch." I carried that phrase with me for years after, a kind of grisly talisman, until I came to this place, L'Lal'lor.

From the beginning the language came easily to me, unlike some of the other anthros who had to struggle with it. All the reports of the histog people

and the geols led us to believe that the Henderson's
IV civs were going to be friendly, unwarlike, and
unthreatened by us, which meant we could take
along only the minimum of military advisers, which
we preferred. Their air was breathable, though it
would take a bit of getting used to, the oxygen count
was a bit thinner than we'd have liked. But given
that our guilds have worked in headhunting territories and societies where torture is an art and
slogged through planets on which giant carnivores
were the closest things to a civilization, Henderson's IV was not a threat. We needed no heavy
artillery to survive.

The first five years, then, we studied their language, folklore, art forms. We listened to tapes of
their songs. Since I'm a pretty fair hand on guitar
and sitar and other strings—ethno-musicology was
my minor at the Academy—I was able to reproduce
some of the songs myself. I've never liked electronic
stuff, which makes me something of a throwback
anyway.

But of course what we were really all working
toward was the time we could go planetside and
face-to-face with the civs.

I was chosen for the first landing because of my
ability with the language and my music and my
knowledge of death-centered societies. I did my the-
sis on tomb imagery in seven First Contact civili-
zations. And maybe I was chosen because I was Dr.
Z's fair-haired boy—oh, I've overheard the whispers. But most of what I've learned about being an
anthro, I've learned from her. I'm not ashamed to
admit it. She's a—a genius, sir. And we thought we
had a pretty fair handle on things.

We set down the skimmer just outside the only city on the planet, L'Lal'dome. The rest of the eastern side of the island continent is a series of small rural villages surrounded by farms and the west is mostly mountains, though there is a rough ridge of hills to the north of 'Dome.

I can read maps, son.

I'm sorry, sir. I didn't mean to imply . . . Well, then we waited.

Following landing plan set by Culture Contact, sir. Sit and wait for the civs so as to appear non-threatening.

Lieutenant, I've been in service longer than you've been able to wipe your nose.

Yes, sir.

It took the better part of a day, but at last a party was sent from the 'Dome to greet us led by a priestess and a company of archers.

Women, sir. All of them.

Don't smirk, Lieutenant. I've been up against matriarchal societies before. And for your information, my first captain, aboard the USS *Malthus*, was a woman.

May I continue, sir? At last the Queen herself arrived, flanked by a group of princes. One—I was later to know him quite well—was brave enough to knock upon the door. They all jumped back when it opened and the stairs dropped down.

All eight of us came out in full landing gear, of course. Not that we needed it. The air had already been tested thoroughly and we all had our inoculations. But usually blocked cultures appreciate ceremony, so we give them the works: costumes, ritual, even magic, then speak to them in their own tongue. It establishes us with the chiefs of state quite quickly.

At the bottom step, Lieutenant Hopfner took off his bubble, stroked his beard, and spoke what we thought were the correct ritual words. We had spent hours debating them.

"I am not an enemy," he said.

The Queen gave a small smile and answered, "Why should you be?"

What he had actually said, it turns out, was, "I am not a quarreling woman." No wonder the Queen responded that way. It was not an auspicious beginning.

No, I don't expect it was. I also don't remember reading about that exchange in any of the lieutenant's notes—and they are vast.

Is that an official reprimand to the lieutenant, sir? Should I include it in the tape?

Include everything for now, Malkin. We will decide later what—if anything—needs to be deleted.

Yes, sir.

Continue, Aaron.

My God, they were beautiful, sir. Our tapes, even our infrareds, had not prepared us for that. They were like something out of the old tales of the Celtic faerie.

Explain that, son.

The Royal women, the Queen especially, are tall, slim, golden-eyed, with masses of long dark wiry hair that refuse to lie quietly but seem almost alive with electricity. They move with a supple dancer's grace. The men are the same, only their hair is trimmed shoulder length and bound down by metal brow bands. They all wear silken clothes whose colors seem to shift and change in every breeze. The priestess is shaven of her hair, but her acolytes are not, and they wear short skirts which show off their legs. They all—Queen, priestess, princes, and acolytes—wear metal bands encrusted with gemstones on their upper arms and at their wrists. Their feet are shod in leather sandals with thongs tied up to the knees.

The women of Arcs and Bow, their warriors—hunters, really, as they seem to fight no wars—are the only ones with short hair. Short and muddy-colored, cut off above the ears. And they are trogs.

Spell that, please. For the records.

Trogs. T-r-o-g-s. Short for troglodytes. That's what Lieutenant Hopfner called them and the name stuck. They are short, maybe five five, squat, bandy-legged, blue-eyed as far as I could tell, well-muscled, broad-shouldered. They have small chins and largish foreheads and seem almost, well, brutish in nature. It's a wonder that the two races—for that is what they are—can interbreed.

Do they?

Yes, Sir. That's what the tapes indicate. The Royal men interbreed with the trog women. They call it *plukenna*, tumbling. When the Royals have intercourse with their own kind, male or female, they call it *ladanna*, touching with joy. But they also have a word which they use interchangeably for both races, *rarredenna*, which means plowing or sowing of the seed. Occasionally the Royals are able to get a tall, slim Royal-looking child on one of the trog women. It is taken away when it reaches puberty and is raised as a Royal in the city of L'Lal'dome. The crossbreeds aren't true Royals. Often they are sterile or they don't breed true; they die younger than their fathers, though they live longer than the trogs.

Is that kind of crossbreeding unusual, Aaron?

Not really, sir. I mean, it's not so different from what we think happened between our early Earth races, fair-skinned and light-haired Neanderthals from the North mingling with darker-skinned Cro Mags from the South. Most of us inbetween types, some archeols say, are the result.

I wasn't really looking for a lecture, son. Yes or no would have done as well.

No, sir. I understand, sir. May I go on?

Do.

We all followed Lieutenant Hopfner's lead and took off our helmets. Our suits were a bit hot, but we were stuck with them for the day, and we followed the Queen and her entourage back into the city. It was quite a walk in our suits with the thin air and all, but we'd been through worse in other places.

It was there that I first met Linni. The Gray Wanderer, sir.

I remember.

She was waiting at the gates, so still and unsmiling and, I thought, infinitely more beautiful than the Queen. The Queen had—I'm not sure if I am remembering this correctly, but it seems to me I noticed it even then—a predatory quality to her beauty. But Linni seemed an armored innocent, armored in silence.

She joined the processional only a step behind the Queen and to the right of the priestess. Behind them ranged the acolytes and princes, and behind them the archers. We were relegated to last place, which was just as well, because we had trouble keeping up. Our line of marchers was fairly ragged by the time we reached the city. Only Hopfner and I didn't fall behind, he because of his long legs and I because of my silly pride.

The city is a maze of streets complicated by market-stands. There were trogs everywhere, but they stood aside when the Queen came through, pulling back almost as if afraid her touch might sear them.

And like a great wave, we rolled along, gathering up flotsam as we went, so that by the time we had reached the palace—a strange building of shell-spackled stone and wooden beams—there were hundreds of people in our wake.

The trogs were stopped by guards at the Queen's Apartments, but we were passed through into a dizzying series of whorled passageways. We went too quickly to map the place and ended up in a great hall that seemed littered with cushions but no other furnishings except drapes.

In the center of the hall was a raised dais and the Queen made for that at once.

Lieutenant Hopfner started after her, but I managed to hold on to his sleeve.

"Wait and let them instruct us," I whispered.

And since I was an Anthro First, he agreed.

The archers meanwhile had ranged themselves around the walls of the room, their wooden bows slung across their backs carelessly. Hopfner had checked that out, I'm sure, before agreeing. The princes had plunked themselves down on the cushions so unobtrusively, it was clear that what had seemed scattered and casual at first glance was a precise and exact floor plan to them. I have no doubt it was made up of carefully calibrated or marked-off territories signifying status.

Two older princes, their mustaches announcing
their age, lay down on the steps that led to the plat-
form. On the highest tier the Queen sank back onto
a profusion of boldly marked pillows, the so-called
thirty cusions of Queenship. At her feet sat the tall,
unsmiling girl in gray. Linni.

The Queen waved the priestess to her. They have
a complicated kind of hand code which we do not
yet fully understand. It seems as quick and supple
as sign language, though it may be quite simple.
Royal to Royal it appears to be conversation, but
when used with servants, it gives the appearance of
command and reply.

Lieutenant, note that as soon as possible I
want videos made of that signing and get some
anthros on it. I don't like my people in a culture
that can converse secretly.

Yes, sir.

"Come to me, strangers from the sky," the
Queen said, her hand wigwagging at us as she spoke.

All eight of us found ourselves firmly escorted to
the base of the dais by the archers. They were very
strong.

Dr. Zambreno and the other anthros bowed their
heads, and reluctantly Hopfner and his aides followed suit. For a moment, though, I forgot my training and stared openly at the tall girl. She stared back
at me for a long golden moment, then slowly looked
at her queen.

"So, you are not a quarreling woman," the
Queen said at last to the lieutenant.

Her people made a strange sound, more a buzz
than a laugh.

"Are you a man?"

"I am," said Hopfner. "But not all of us are."
He made a broad gesture toward us, careful to keep
it slow and wide and nonthreatening.

"Show me which is which," demanded the
Queen.

"The men will stand by me, the women will stand
over there," he said.

We followed his instructions, which meant we
were four and four. We had thought that, with a
strong matriarchy, it was best to keep our numbers
even. We were also four anthros and four military,
but that difference was not immediately apparent.

"Why does a man lead?" asked the Queen.

"It is our way to share the lead, man and
woman," said Hopfner.

"It is not *our* way."

There was another buzz stir around us, a small
undercurrent of whispers, as the princes shifted on
their cushions. Then the Queen raised her hand and
there was an immediate silence. The only one in the
room who had not stirred noticeably during that exchange was the girl at the Queen's feet.

Lieutenant Hopfner bowed his head again. He
knew that he was in troubled waters, moving over
into anthro territory.

"Come up to me. Here," the Queen demanded,
pointing to Hopfner.

He hesitated a moment and I whispered, "Move
slowly, Lieutenant. And go only to the step below
the top riser. No further unless she directs it."

He grunted a response and moved up the stairs
carefully. When he reached the next-to-the-top step,
he stopped. He was then between the two older
princes who reached up simultaneously and touched
his hands, indicating that he should kneel. He did

it stiffly, reluctance showing in his rigid backbone
and the way his hands remained unmoving at his
sides.

The Queen ran her fingers lightly across his face,
almost as if she were blind, seeing him with her
fingertips. Her hands lingered on his beard and the
lines around his eyes the longest. Then, with a flick,
she dismissed him. The princes tugged at his suit,
and he backed down the stairs.

"You!" the Queen said, pointing this time at me.

Having watched Hopfner's performance, I knew
what to do. I went up the stairs slowly as if I were
a dancer, and when I reached the next-to-last tier,
I went down on one knee but kept my face turned
up toward the Queen.

You dance, do you, son?

A little, sir. It's part of our training, folk dancing.
But ritual moves are much the same, culture to culture. We practice them in school. They are much
more fluid than military movements, though equally
precise. The lieutenant moved as an aggressor
would, and the Queen sensed it immediately. And
she found something on his face—age, perhaps—
that she didn't like. I made my body language promise fealty-of-the-moment, an invitation to explora-
tion.

Well, her fingers fairly danced across my face. I
come from a soft-skinned family anyway, and I am
younger by fifteen years than the lieutenant, twenty
years younger than Dr. N'Jymnbo, and a bit
younger than the military attaché. The L'Lal'lorian
culture favors young men in some things, so I naturally became the favored one of our group. The
Queen signaled me to sit at her feet by the girl Linni.

Then the Queen examined each of us in turn, though she was frustrated by the seamless suits and puzzled by the metal zippers and clasps.

The lieutenant later commented that it had been like being fingered by a herd of monkeys.

Paula Sigman, our Anthro Second, corrected him.

"Troop," she said.

Hopfner looked surprised.

"Monkeys come in troops."

We had a good laugh at that since, as the lieutenant pointed out, the trogs did look like monkeys and they *were* the military. Sort of. But that came later, when we were back in the ship for the night. First nights planetside are usually full of such bad jokes and small puns. We need laughter to settle us down, I guess.

You said that was later, Aaron. What else happened in the Queen's room? Was there entertainment? Did you give them gifts?

We didn't bring gifts because our studies of the tapes had indicated that the L'Lal'lorians were not a gift-giving people. Except at times of grieving, in the Halls, there was little exchange of monies or presents. Rather they paid for things with a kind of elaborate bartering system and the Royals paid for things with public touching and private tumbling and the ultimate gift of a Royal-bred child. Also, it is a recent Anthro Central policy not to bring gifts.

Is that a regulation? I have no record of it.

Not exactly a regulation, sir. Just a policy, though with time it may become reg. We call it the Manhattan Policy. A recent Funded Study showed that such transfers of gifts, like the ancient buying of the island of Manhattan on Earth leads only to misunderstandings and misappropriations and years of bad feelings. So—no gifts. Of course, since it's policy and not reg, we can bend it a bit if necessary.

Sir, should I get all of this down?

All of it, Malkin.

They fed us with sweet fruits and cakes and tumblers of a honey-based wine. It was very mild. And we were each supplied with a couple of pillows apiece and had to lie down on them for eating. The lieutenant and his aides seemed uncomfortable, but we anthros fared well enough, even in our landing suits. After learning to eat raw invertebrates while kneeling for hours on the shells with the *jung!* GRAN'OTYLI, cushions and sweet succulents were a pleasure. I did my training under Dr. Z on *jung!*

The Queen herself peeled grapelike sweets for me, but she let Linni teach me how to eat them. If you bite into one quickly, it releases a bitter spurt which even the sweet aftertaste does not erase. But if you first roll it around your mouth for a moment, then squeeze gently with your lips, the juice runs back into your mouth and is incredibly sweet with just a taste of tart. The grapes are called *loro'pae.*

Then Prince B'oremos sang for us. After about three or four songs, I asked to see the instrument. It was a plecta, not too different from our mandolin in looks, but with a surprisingly deep tone. I experimented with several runs up and down the fretted neckboard and won a startled, shy, beginning smile from Linni.

Emboldened, I asked the Queen if I might sing for her.

"What can you sing, sky-wanderer?" she asked.

"I can sing one or two of your songs, my lady," I said. Actually I had about thirty of them in my repertoire but most were their sacred grief songs and not appropriate. "And many more of our own."

She mused a bit, then said, "I know all of our songs and they interest me not in the least in the mouth of a man from the sky. But what kind of songs do your people grieve with?"

"We sing many kinds of songs," I said, "and only a few of them are for grief. We also sing for love."

"What is this word?" she asked, for I had said *love* in English since they hadn't the word for it.

"It is like—and unlike—your ladanna."

There was a sharp intake of breath in the room and I wondered if I had misspoken, using a taboo word. Yet there had been nothing in the tapes to indicate that. Perhaps the problem was not with us but with the trogs in the room.

"What do you, sky-farer, know of ladanna?" the Queen asked.

I looked over at Dr. Z. She moved her hand back and forth as if to caution me to tread with care.

"I know . . ." I began. "I know that it is like—and unlike—plukenna."

The Queen was silent for a moment, but Linni spoke.

"There is a story, one of the lesser tales, that talks of that difference," she said. "For it was and it was not that a Queen wanted to know whether it was better to be plowed by a Common Griever or to be sown by a prince. But she knew there was none but a prince past his mission year who could touch her without being consumed by the fire in her skin. So she lay down in the sand and commanded the waves to wash over her and put her fires out.

Well, the waters lapped her head and shoulder all that day and the next, but still her skin was hot and dry to the touch. So she went deeper even beneath the waves. Little colored fish swam in between her fingers and seashells washed through the dark ropes of her hair. But still her skin was dry and hot. So she went deeper still till the water washed away her skin and hair and she was nothing but a ligature of bones that neither prince nor commoner could plow. She was grieved by all but sown again by none, so for her, plukenna and ladanna became one and the same. For no one else are they even similar."

I nodded. "We have a song about the difference ourselves," I said. I began the old ballad of 'Tam Lin,' explaining the story to them as I sang, about the fairy Queen and the girl Fair Janet, both of whom were sown by the young knight Tam Lin. But of course the ending was unsatisfactory to them, for the human girl wins back her own true love from the Queen. I was about halfway through the song when I knew I was going to be in trouble by the end, so I let it trail off.

"Your song does not please me, for it has unpleasant sounds and no real ending, but your singing is pleasant enough," said the Queen. "Is that a song not of grieving but of . . . What was your word?"

"Love," said Dr. Z, standing slowly and moving forward with the easy practiced grace of an anthro, though she weighs close to three hundred pounds. I saw that she had, in the interval of my song, taken the pins out of her hair and it fell in long spirals over her back, down to her waist. There were heavy gray streaks running through the black, which makes her hair even more striking. She has used that trick often with humanoid civs. Have you read her paper on

that? It's brilliant! She stood at the bottom of the
dais and bowed her head, letting the hair come forward over her shoulders.

"You are one of those who sometimes leads?"
asked the Queen.

"I am," Dr. Z said and looked up. She was careful not to smile. "Our boys sing almost as nicely as
yours, but of course our songs talk of different
things. We are a different people."

"From the sky," said the Queen.

"Where love is—and is not—the same as it is
here on your world," Dr. Z said.

"Run along, boy," said the Queen, dismissing me
with short, quick flicks of her hand. "I would speak
to your Queen."

We have a full account of Dr. Z's notes, sir.

I've read them. Seems the two "Queens"
talked of ruling the trogs and a bit of history and
pretty young boys, but no more specifically about
Aaron Spenser. And since it is with Anthro First
Class Spenser we are concerned, I see no need
to read it into the official record, Lieutenant.

As you wish, sir.

I was sent away with the others in the charge of
Linni, who showed us around the apartments and
who entertained us in a little courtyard with still
more food. And though the lieutenant was worried
about Dr. Z, worried that we were slowly being split
up, nothing bad came of it. In fact, everyone was
very pleasant to us; there was an aura of gentleness
and good breeding about it all. No one's voice was
ever raised above a whisper. I think it was *that* that
bothered Hopfner the most. He said afterward a
good shout once in a while might purge them.

Thinking back on it, I guess what they desperately needed was to laugh. But perhaps for them laughing was sacrilegious, like telling a dirty joke in a convent.

Around dark, which seems to seep in slowly around the edges of the sky like long black fingers pointing toward the palace, we were summoned by the Queen. And after much ritual bowing and signing, we were escorted back to the ship. Dr. Z had us give report, which is not so different from what I'm telling you now, except for the use of technical terms which defined the anthropological aspects. Dr. Z coordinated our notes with Hopfner's.

We have those, sir.

And she told me that I handled myself well under pressure. She did warn me, however, that more pressures were likely to be exerted—on me in particular. And by the Queen.

"She sees young, sweet-faced boys as her own private hunting grounds, Aaron," Dr. Z said. "And as she is not now grieving anyone important and has nothing better to think about, she is just as likely to want to try you. But be careful. That story the girl told has some truth to it. The Queen held my hand at one point, sister to sister, Queen to Queen, and after a minute, I could feel her skin growing noticeably hotter on mine. A long touch brings it out. Their metabolism is probably very different from ours."

"I'll take care," I said seriously.

She winked at me, and we both laughed.

We went the next day without our heavy suits. The lieutenant and his aides wore dress blues, which were still too hot for the planet. Dr. Z had the anthros dress in white shorts and short-sleeve shirts.

Because of her weight—though she said it was because she was our Queen!—Dr. Z wore one of the
silky baptism robes from *jung!* instead. The back of
her robe was embroidered with a red lizardlike creature, the famous "dragons" or morgs of *jung!*,
though they are really more like eels and live un-
derwater. Of course the Queen wanted the robe but
Dr. Z did not give it to her, though she let her borrow
it for a day. The next morning the Queen had an
exact duplicate, or as close a copy as L'Lal'lorian
hands could come. Evidently six apprentice grievers, all artists, stayed up the night working on the
embroidery.

Didn't that violate your Manhattan Policy?

Dr. Z didn't actually *give* the robe to the Queen,
sir. She lent it. And got it back.

You seem to have a problem distinguishing
between the letter and the spirit of the law, son.

It's not exactly a law, sir.

Hmmm. There seems to be more than one way
to contaminate a culture. Perhaps the wrong person is on trial here. Strike that, Lieutenant. Just
my musing.

Let me say, sir, that any contact is a kind of contamination. That's the first corollary to the Anthro
Oath—"to observe, to study, to learn," is what we
say. But we know that anytime you study a culture
face-to-face, by the very act of studying, you change
it. It's known as Mead's Law, sir.

That's like Heisenberg, sir.

Lieutenant, why don't you keep *your* musings
to yourself. That way they won't contaminate
mine.

Yes, sir.

The point is to keep the contamination as insignificant as possible and to always understand in what way the culture under study has changed because of the contact. I hope that you'll come to see that it was I—not the culture—that was the most changed.

That, son, will certainly come into our final judgment.

While the Queen and Dr. Z continued their talk, the rest of us went exploring in other ways. Dr. Z had given us assignments, which we were—within limits set by the civs—supposed to carry out. I was to try to visit the Hall of Grief because of my interest in artistic expression. It was my luck to be accompanied by B'oremos, the Singer of Dirges, as he was called.

The prince who had sung for you the day before?

Yes, sir. He took me first to his own rooms where he was fussed over endlessly by a group of trog servants. While they did his hair and nails, I examined the instrument collection he had hanging on his walls. They were all stringed and fretted. In fact, except for the funerary drums, some very minor reedlike pipes, and bells used to announce visitors to and from the Queen, the strings were the only musical instruments on the planet. It was an art form in a very early stage, though the music B'oremos could coax from those strings was impressive.

He bade me choose an instrument to play that day and after almost an hour of trying them, I ended up with something called a harmonus. It was shaped more or less like an ancient Indian instrument, the sitar, with a wide hollow-sounding bowl carved from a gourd and a three-foot-long neck strung with seven strings. I liked the odd modalities of the thing and adopted it for my own.

Once during that hour, when I was sitting with the harmonus in my lap—you had to play it sitting—the tune I picked out was so strange I laughed out loud.

B'oremos looked over at me from the pillow where his servants were still working on his face. "That is a peculiar harsh sound you make."

I apologized. "I am not yet used to this last string," I said, pointing to the wide drone string that ran only half the length of the harmonus.

"I am talking of the grating noise you made with your mouth, like the sound of moons' caps snapping closed."

I laughed again.

"There," he said, pointing at me. His servants bowed and elbowed one another. He dismissed them irritatedly with his hands.

"It is a laugh," I said. "Do your people not laugh at all?"

He shrugged back with a wry, small smile. "We are men of tears. To grieve well is an art."

"We are men without tears," I said. "We try not to grieve at all."

"Well, Man Without Tears," he said, "then it is time to take you to the Hall of Grief. There we will find the tears in you as easily as you find the music in that." He pointed languidly at the harmonus, which I shifted from my lap.

He shouted, and a new servant entered on silent feet.

"This is Mar-keshan," said my host. "He is to servants what the Queen is to women."

Mar-keshan bowed, read his master's fingers, and with quick flicks of his own fingers silently answered back. I liked Mar-keshan at once. He was brisk, almost to the point of brusqueness. His round face was a berry brown, his eyes the bleached-out blue of a sailor's, the kind that gives a double impression—that of blindness but of far-seeing as well.

"Dress him for the Hall," said B'oremos. I had a feeling he was speaking aloud for my sake, his fingers having already given those same orders.

Before I could stop him, Mar-keshan was gone, then came back again with a golden chiton of a flowing silklike material.

"It is the color of your hair and skin, A'ron," said B'oremos.

I was certain that it was the discussion of that color that had occupied their hands before.

The two stripped me down and slipped me into the outfit. It had a band of material that went over my right shoulder, covered my chest, and fit down at the waist with a drawstring tie. The skirt fell in soft folds to my thighs. Thank God I was slim or it would have been positively obscene.

Mar-keshan marveled at my shorts, and my underpants made him gasp in admiration. They obviously had no experience with elasticized waistbands. They traded my underclothes for a silken loincloth that was uncomfortably tight. All the while they chattered silently with semaphoring fingers. I could not even guess at their comments.

None of the prince's sandals fit and I had to make do with a pair of Mar-keshan's old leather slippers. Neither of them was happy with that makeshift, but they both agreed that my own boots were totally unsuitable.

With that, I shouldered the harmonus and B'oremos took up his plecta, and we went off to the Hall.

You must have looked a sight, son.

What I looked was a bit Greek, I guess. But it's something we train for, native costumes. And as such things go, it was really rather elegant, if a bit small and scanty. I knew some of the anthros who first opened up the moons of Chancery, and they had to wear a coating of dung and mud to help celebrate the birth days of the native chiefs. And one friend of mine trained on Landon's X, where the intelligent species wore metal coats made of nails, points in, to indicate humility. A silk skirt however short is hardly a hardship in comparison, sir.

Ha-ha. I like your attitude, Aaron. Now—tell me about the Hall.

The building itself is of the same shell-encrusted gray-and-white stone as the palace, only where the palace is mammoth and overbalanced by a pair of mismatched towers, there is something elegant and fragile and lonely about the Hall. It has pillars in the front that are covered with carvings of such intricacy I could not decipher them; "metaphors of grief," was all that B'oremos said when I asked. There is also a relief of some kind splayed out under a gabled roof. The whole thing is over two stories high, but it seems at once smaller and larger than that. There are thirteen stone steps leading to the doors.

The doors are of some kind of heavy wood, also carved, and those carvings I *did* decipher, for they are mostly of weeping women and skeletons set on high-rising biers.

We pushed through the heavy doors and went inside. I had expected it to be dark, but to my surprise the hall was quite bright. One side of the roof was open, though at night or in the case of bad weather it evidently could be shuttered. Open windows let in the fluttering sea breezes.

Tables were everywhere. It was like a mad indoor marketplace, with sellers crying their wares, only their wares were all free, artifacts of grief. Mourners scurried up and down the jigsaw-puzzle aisles, choosing to listen to a singer here or a poet there, pausing to watch a magician make kerchiefs with the names of dead kin appear and disappear at will. If you stood still for a single moment, someone would be at your elbow trying to bring you immortality for a sister or brother or mother.

Not for a father?

That's a problem, sir. These people have little concept of fatherhood—except in a general sense. It's never really clear who has fathered what child, as they seem to make love indiscriminately because the men have such a short time of . . . of potency. Five years at most and then their reproductive organs shrivel and are reabsorbed into the body.

Half a year of ship time. That's a hell of a thought.

B'oremos and I stood apart from the mob for a while, just watching. He seemed somewhat removed from the proceedings, as if he had trouble becoming really involved. And I—I just wanted to sort through my impressions. It seemed that though we were *in* the Hall of Grief, I was not hearing any grieving, which was what I had been led to expect. It was all form and formality; there seemed to be little of real substance. No tears, no breast beat-

ing, no—no real sadness. I was about to put that
question to B'oremos when the entire Hall suddenly
hushed as if on cue and all eyes looked toward a
stage that ran halfway around the western wall.

Linni walked out on the stage, moving with a
pride of bearing that the greatest actresses would
envy. "Here I am," her body seemed to say. "I
have much to tell you."

She came to the exact center of the stage, a plumb
line for the emotions of the crowd, and waited an
extra beat of silence. Then, as if gathering the mourners' silence to her, to reinforce her own, she began
to speak/sing/chant the opening of their great Song
of the Seven Grievers, the prose poem about their
Creation.

What I had not known was that we had arrived
at the eve of a new season, the season of Rarre-
dennikon, sowing time. And except for the death of
the Queen herself, at which time the Queen's Own
Griever would naturally be in deep mourning, the
festival was a time of cessation of grief. The festival
began with the recitation of this poem. Our landing
at this particular time had been a fluke, but it could
become significant if the civs chose to see it as some
sort of sign.

The poem that Linni spoke was long. It took over
an hour of straight recital. But not once did she falter
or stop for water, or cough or clear her throat. That
straight, dark-haired girl stood center stage and held
us all with her presence and the power of the words.
The only break came when she spoke the *Selah*, or
"Amen," or however we might translate it. In their
language the word is *Arrush*. It means, basically,
"so be it." Then the Hall echoed her.

"Arrush" came the wave of sound back, washing over her.

She paused, gathered in the silence that followed the sound, and began again.

I had heard the tapes of another Master Griever instructing the apprentices in the recitation of this same poem. In fact, I had learned great portions of it myself and I had puzzled out its meaning, both the literal translation and the cultural implications. But the tapes had not given a hint of the power the spoken story had. Or at least as it was spoken by Linni. She swept us away. I do not think that I moved, except to say the Arrush, until she was done. I didn't feel the weight of the harmonus on my shoulder or the tightness of the loincloth or the too small slippers on my feet. I was, quite simply, mesmerized by both the teller and the tale.

And when it was over, and she was greeted by the last great Arrush, she raised her hands to her eyes, the ritual sign of weeping. I had tears in my eyes as well, but I wiped them away at once, though B'oremos, who had been watching me rather than the stage saw me do it.

"Now we can sing," he said, taking me by the elbow and moving me toward the stage. He swiped some succulents from a table and pressed one into my mouth. "You remember how to eat this?"

I nodded, letting the grapey fruit roll about between my lips and then, with the juice spurting backward into my mouth, I followed him onto the stage.

We traded songs for about an hour, he singing a variety of songs about sowing that were surprisingly unbawdy given the amount of detail they conjured up. I gave them "Barbara Allen," "The Twa Sisters," and "The Great Selchie of Sule Skerry," though the translations were stories I made up on the spot. Then because of the encouragement the crowd gave me, I sang "Little Musgrave," "Mary Hamilton," and "The Bonny Earl of Murray" as well.

I'm not familiar with any of those songs, son.

They're all old English folk ballads, sir. My specialty.

B'oremos introduced me as the Man Without Tears and that was what I was called from then on. A'ron, coincidentally, means A Man Without. Their entire name for me was A'Ron'lordur. Actually they called all of us Aer'Ron'lordurren, Men (People) Without Tears. And I teased B'oremos about that, saying that it read, in our language, more like Lords from the Air. He liked that. He and the other princes are very fond of word games. And later Linni, poet that she was, called me her Lord of Air and Sky. She had asked me what her name seemed like in our tongue and I told her it reminded me of the linnet, a little singing bird from my home world. She wrote a poem to me called "The Bird Sings to the Lord of Air and Sky." It does not translate particularly well, but it goes something like this:

> The boughs are heavy with song.
> I would make each note
> An arrow to pierce your heart.
> Grieve for me, young lord,
> When I am earth and you are sky
> And only the syllables of song
> Dropping like rain, rising like dew
> between.

Of course in their language both the first words and the last words of each line rhyme, and the word she chose for "between" is the middle syllable of both earth and sky. So the poem is infinitely more complex than the simple word-for-word translation shows. And she composed it on the spot.

After the hour, B'oremos and I left the stage, though it was afterward filled constantly with changing acts: dancers, singers, mimes, costumers posing in elaborate tableaux, magicians, jugglers. All the performances were dedicated to the ushering-in of the season of sowing. And though the mood seemed elevated, without laughter it did not seem particularly happy, but that, of course, is an alien and subjective point of view.

B'oremos took me by the hand and led me up and down aisles. We sampled many different kinds of food and drink. Their wines are much sweeter than ours, being honey-based, and it takes a good deal more drinking to get drunk. Perhaps their berries don't ferment as readily as ours. But the fruits and breads were wonderful after so many years on board ship, and the meats were served in tiny bite-sized portions, coated with piquant sauces. I was forever licking my fingers and nodding to those who offered food to me. B'oremos told me that if I were especially pleased, I should offer caresses— "touches"—in exchange. I gave a few tentative hugs to some of the younger trog girls and afterward they were swamped with customers, so I guess public recognition *was* a viable form of payment. After that I was a great deal freer with my hands.

Finally I turned to B'oremos. "But when do they grieve?"

"When there is someone to grieve for," he said, his face speaking elaborately of my innocence.

Later back in the Queen's hall, I was asked what I thought of my tour of the Hall of Grief and I made a crucial mistake. Perhaps the wine had affected me more than I knew or perhaps I was just not sufficiently careful with the knowledge I had. I said, "I was very impressed with the singing and dancing within the Hall, and especially with your Master Griever. But since I had been told it was the Queen's Own Hall of Grief, I expected grieving and there was little to be seen."

The Queen smiled slowly.

"B'oremos tells me," I went on, encouraged by her smile, "that you grieve only when there is someone for whom to grieve. Is that so?"

"Man Without Tears," said the Queen in a low voice, "do you really wish to hear us grieve?"

"I do," I said.

Linni, sitting at the Queen's feet gasped and put her hand to her mouth.

"Then we shall grieve for you and yours. Tomorrow." The Queen dismissed us as far as the bottom steps.

Our entire party stood waiting almost at attention while the Queen conferred with B'oremos, whispering into his ear and fingering his hands with quick little taps. Then she drew back from him and pulled a small silken bag from deep within the bosom of her dress. With great ceremony, she handed it to him and dismissed him. He crawled backward down the stairs, standing gracefully when he reached the bottom.

"A'ron," said the Queen in a cozening manner, "will you stay this evening with me?"

"He has work to do back at the ship," said Dr. Z, though she used the word for tower instead of ship. "Silver Tower" and "Sky Tower" were their names for our skimmer.

"Let him speak for himself," said the Queen.

I looked from Dr. Z to the Queen and back again, then glanced at Linni, whose hand still rested on her lips. When I turned back to the Queen, her mouth was slightly open and her eyes seemed preternaturally bright. The lines from "Tam Lin" suddenly ran through my mind: "Out then spak the Queen of Fairies/And an angry woman was she . . ."

I bowed my head. "I fear that I have too much to do, though it would be an honor to spend such time with the Queen and to learn of L'Lal'dor from her own lips."

"Then give them the purse," the Queen said coldly.

B'oremos bowed and handed the silken pocket to Dr. Z.

"There are three Lumin nuts in here," he explained, "from the Queen's own personal trees. Dissolved in wine, the nuts provoke dreams of such *loving*, as you say, that you shall never know the like. Her Majesty gives these to you with the thoughts and wishes of her people."

Dr. Z bowed back and took up the little silken purse, weighing it in her hand. "We thank you for your generosity but wonder how and in what manner we might repay it."

"You will know in the morning," said the Queen. "B'oremos will prepare the Cup when you invite him in."

"I don't like it," said Hopfner the moment we had closed the door of the ship, carefully locking the archers outside.

"Of course you don't," said Dr. Z. She turned in a fury on me. "And you, young man, you positively invited it. You *know* they believe in ritual euthanasia. And you *know* the significance of the Lumin nuts. If I do not drink them, the Queen will withdraw from us and that means five years of research thrown away, not to mention massive cultural contamination if their commoners see that one can reject the Queen's expressed offer of the Lumin."

"She didn't specify who should drink," I said. "Let me do it. I deserve it. It was my fault. I accept the consequences." I held out my hand for the silk bag.

"Oh, don't be stupid!" said Dr. Z. "I'm angry and I'd like to throttle you with my bare hands. But with me, saying that is as far as I go. The L'Lal'lorian Queen, however, has a much bolder power of expression and a millennium of cultural imperative behind it. Don't go making similar offers to her. Aaron."

"I advise we simply lift off." Hopfner rolled the edges of his beard between his fingers.

"And I advise you to remember that I outrank you, *Lieutenant*." Dr. Z's voice was cool. "And as Chief Anthro, I have to outthink you on these matters." Then she chuckled. "I outweigh you, too." She upended the purse and dumped the kernels onto the table. They looked like wrinkled, hard peppercorns. "Not very lethal looking, are they? I'm tempted to have them ground up over my salad."

"I wouldn't advise that without a test," put in N'Jymnbo. As medical officer he was efficient, though he lacked any sense of the outrageous, which, according to Dr. Z, was why he had never advanced very far in our Guild.

Strike that last, Lieutenant.

It's out, sir.

Thank you, sir. I'm not sure why I let that slip.

Dr. Z continued to push the nuts around on the table as she mused. "I'm willing to bet that three nuts, while lethal to someone the size of their Queen, would hardly touch me, as I have about one hundred seventy or so pounds on her. It would probably mean a bad night—and nothing more."

"In fact, you don't know *how* your metabolism would handle that," cautioned N'Jymnbo.

"Don't worry, N'Jymnbo. If I pull through, it will be just as bad culturally as if I hadn't taken the Lumin at all. Probably start a whole new religion: Fat Is Beautiful."

I laughed.

"I vote we feed the nuts to Aaron," said Clark. As Hopfner's right hand, she was always first to agree with him or to make his less agreeable statements aloud.

I looked at Hopfner's face. He was smiling grimly.

Dr. Z picked up the nuts one at a time. "Since when," she said cheerfully, "is a ship's company a democracy? The only vote that really counts here is mine. After all, Her Royal High Mucky-Muck gave these nuts to me, Queen to Queen." She chuckled. "And believe me, I'm not planning to die to satisfy either Aaron's curiosity or the Queen's pleasure. I have other plans for my old age. But I am thinking that some kind of stratagem, some kind of sleight of hand, would be welcome here. N'Jymnbo, what *are* you carrying in that medkit of yours?"

N'Jymnbo took the white medkit from around his neck and spread it open before us. It contained a limited supply of bandages, bone plaster, one pair of forceps, three scalpels, some spray anesthesia, disposable syringes, and a couple of ampoules of morphix.

Dr. Z fingered the ampoules and laughed out loud. "Well, well, what we have here, my friends, is the makings of a fairy tale scenario."

Hopfner and his three aides gawped, but we anthros were used to Dr. Z's pronouncements. She has an antic sense of humor, a broad reading knowledge of cultures, and her specialty is Old Earth Analogues.

"Imagine, if you will," she began in her tale-telling voice, "a three-hundred-pound Snow White tended by her devoted seven dwarfs."

Only I understood the reference immediately.

Better let me in on it, too, son.

It's a class 2 Mythic Structure, sir. Motif #37 in the Index: rescue of sleeping princess. Supplemental Motif #13, Fairy Companions, in this case seven dwarfs.

Is it important to . . . Oh, never mind. Just continue your story.

It's important to understand Dr. Z's plan, sir, which was brilliant. But I think you can get a rough idea of it even without understanding the full implications of the fairy tale trappings.

Then I'll do with the "without."

"Well, Doc," Dr. Z said to N'Jymnbo, "can you put me into transsleep with these things?" She fingered one ampoule and fixed the doctor with a caramel-colored eye. "I want to be as far down as any colonist on a long haul transship."

"It's slightly dangerous, Z. With your weight problems and—"

"I've had my so-called weight problems forever, N'Jymnbo. And I've climbed mountains in the Sigel Range and descended into the slime pits of the Outer CanFields. I may huff and puff more than your average anthro, but I get there. Never mind my weight problem, we have a more immediate problem, the one that Dopey here . . ."

Dopey?

I'm glad *you* asked, Lieutenant.

She meant me, sir. That's one of the names of the dwarfs in a visual variant of the Snow White tale. That was Dr. Z's sense of humor.

D-o-p-e-y. Got it.

"This new problem is the one we have to deal with now."

"Please, Dr. Z, let *me* take the morphix." I reached out, touching her on the arm.

She let my hand remain on her arm; in fact, she covered it with her own hand and looked intently at me. "Aaron, you're a pretty boy, as the Queen would say, but you'd make a terrible Snow White. Besides, there are three things you'd best start remembering; that is, if you want to become a *great* anthro, as I think you do."

"I do, Dr. Z."

"First, stop being such a damned romantic about these cultures. They are—simply—cultures. Not better or worse than the one you grew up with, only different. And sometimes the same. Remember— analogues! Second, start thinking before speaking, which means reduce your protracted adolescent twittiness to an acceptable minimum. And three, do your job and let others do theirs." She turned to

Hopfner. "The difficult part will be convincing that prince, B'oremos, to accept our Cup of Sleep instead of his. *That* is a purely anthro problem, so you and your advisers better clean your weapons or whatever it is you do before bedtime. Let me and mine make final plans."

Of course Hopfner wouldn't accept that and so all eight of us sat down for the discussion, which ranged half the night. But in the end it was clear that as angry as Dr. Z had been about what had happened—what I had done—she accepted the next step easily, that of putting it right by means of an elaborate performance. I think she positively looked forward to her own "death."

For your information, Aaron, all anthros score remarkably high on acting ability in the Morigi-Coville Test. I suspect that the best actors in the known universe are anthropologists.

Thank you, sir. I take that as a compliment.

I'm not sure I meant it as a compliment, but take it any way you please. Only go on.

We slept only a few hours at best and were awakened by the ringing of the breakfast alarms and the smell of fresh caf in the air vents.

At the table, Dr. Z complained. "The only problem with playing Snow White is that N'jymnbo won't let me have anything to eat or drink this morning. And suddenly I'm starved. Imagine playing a deathbed scene with stomach arumble." She reached over to touch one of the little protein cakes and N'Jymnbo slapped her hand away.

"Things are going to be tricky enough without your appetite complicating things, Z," he said. "Be a good girl."

"Not even a lick of frosting?"

"Not even."

She sighed loudly, which made us all laugh a bit nervously. At that she looked around and winked at me. "Stage fright, kids?" she asked, adding something strange, a reference that none of us really caught but made her laugh. "Well, we've got the barn, so let's put on a show."

Then she stood. She was wearing another of her vast robes from *jung!* having set aside the borrowed silk from the Queen. This one was a dark green and the back was embroidered with great tsunamis, white-capped and ferocious. She had braided her hair and the white streaks patterned ribbonlike through the plaits. Standing, arms spread, she looked magnificent, like an ancient Hawaiian queen, one of whose nobility was measured by her vast girth.

We had decided to dress in our landing gear again so that we all would look the same, though we left the bubble helmets aboard ship. And quite a party we made, with Dr. Z descending the silver stairs first, her green caftan billowing and the seven awkward silver-clad attendants behind.

We marched in unison to the strumming of my guitar, which was quite a feat considering the bulk of the landing suits. The last two out of the ship, Hopfner's two male aides, carried out Dr. Z's hammock and frame.

B'oremos met us at the bottom of the stairs and bowed his head. The archers with him inclined their heads as well. But Linni, whom I had not seen at first, for she had been standing to one side, did not move. She held a delicately faceted stone chalice in her hands.

Come, sweet Death, I thought, a fragment of another old song running through my mind. I walked up to her, slinging my guitar over my back as I went.

"The Queen's Own Cup." Her voice was so soft I almost missed what she said. She held the Cup out to me and I saw that her hands trembled.

I put my own hands over hers to steady them for a moment and she looked up into my eyes. Her eyes were golden, but not a clear amber like B'oremos's or the Queen's. Rather they were flecked with a darker gold and there was a ring of that darker color around each iris.

"For your Queen," she said.

"We do not have Queens."

"And you do not have plukenna or ladanna but something else. And you do not grieve," she said to me, so quietly no one else remarked it. "So—I do not think that your Queen should take this Cup." She looked down quickly. It was the most awful heresy she might have spoken.

I bit my lip and hastened to assure her, to stem the tide of contamination that threatened to overwhelm her. "Do not be afraid, Linni. Believe me, all will be well. Our . . . Dr. Z takes this Cup willingly."

"Then I will grieve for her, your not-Queen," said Linni, still speaking to the ground, "your Dot'der'tsee. I will grieve for her as if she were my own."

I smiled at her bowed head, then remembered the ritual in time. "May your lines of mourning be long."

"May her time of dying be short."

While Linni and I had been speaking, hand on hand, Dr. Z had been playing out a different scenario with B'oremos. She accepted her dragon caftan back from him, handing it on to Paula with a queenly gesture. Then she told him that while she valued the Queen's Lumin nuts, in her own world there was a substance that was far better for a queen of her— and she gestured to her body—vastness.

B'oremos took this in, head cocked to one side, then nodded.

Dr. Z signaled and N'Jymnbo brought out the great glass beaker he used for measurements. The incised red lines and numbers glowed in the sunlight, and the half liter of morphix-laced apple juice was prismatic, casting rainbows onto the ship's side.

Dr. Z raised the beaker high and spoke sonorously in Standard English a wonderful mixture of old Earth poetry, the punchline of a robot joke, one of the famed Duncan translations of the *jung!* Rubiyats, and a smattering of other things I didn't quite catch:

> Twas brillig and the slithy toves
> Cast in the fire of Spring!
> Double, double, toil and trouble
> Ask not for whom bells ring.
> For if I forget Jerusalem
> Upon my silent stalk
> Let my tongue cleft, my cunning hand
> Forget now how to walk.

She added in the tongue of L'Lal'lor:

> And if I die before I wake,

> Ashes to ashes, dust to dust
> I pray the Lord my soul to take,
> Let all robots come to rust.

Then she drank the beaker straight down.

I'd heard her use the same muddled verse before, because it sounds wonderful when declaimed, and she's got one of those full operatic voices that can be heard even in the back of a large hall.

"What is a soul?" Linni whispered to me.

Caught up in the drama, I almost answered her but stopped myself in time. "That I am not allowed to say. It is a secret part of our own beliefs." That's the standard anthro line.

She did not ask again but merely watched as Dr. Z sank down onto the hammock, handing N'Jymnbo the beaker. She settled against the pillows. We'd cannibalized all the bed linen on the skimmer, each giving up our own pillows and inflating twenty more from the store of flotation devices. It was a strange and uncomfortable mix, but it did not bother Dr. Z for long. Morphix works quickly, slowing the breathing down at once; soon the other vital signs follow . . .

Son, I've ferried more colonists around star systems than you've got hairs. Don't teach me what I already know. Tell me what I don't know.

Sorry, sir.

As Dr. Z began to lose consciousness, she motioned me over to her and spoke in English.

"Give me a great send-off, Aaron. And remember, don't be a romantic. A good anthro observes, studies, learns. He does not go native—without a reason." Then in the tongue of L'Lal'lor she added,

"You will make them remember me?" and closed her eyes.

I stayed kneeling by her side, for that was what we had practiced. I even murmured back to her, "Dr. Z, I will."

From behind me I heard Linni's low voice say, "May your time of dying be short." B'oremos echoed her.

At that very moment, Dr. Z "died."

N'Jymnbo reached over, picked up her wrist, and counted the imperceptible pulse, then pronounced her dead. We all set up a wailing, a ululation, or at least we anthros did. Hopfner and his three were stiff and rather unconvincing, I thought. They howled and threw themselves to their knees, or rather Clark and the two younger guards fell down. Hopfner stood at attention and worked his jaw convulsively as if in great emotional distress.

But of course not a one of us cried.

B'oremos put his hand on Dr. Z's forehead and his fingers wandered as unobtrusively as possible to below her nose but he could feel no breath. Linni put her palm on Dr. Z's vast bosom but what respirations continued were, of course, so shallow as to be imperceptible.

I stood. "We do not strip our corpses or set them out on pyre and pylon for the birds," I said, keeping my voice tight as if with grief. "Though we shall, of course, leave Dr. Z's body here for all your people to see before we take her back aboard and set her in a transparent casket for viewing." I took a deep breath. Here was the troublesome part, for she would need to be encapsulated in the transsleep unit within seventy-two hours. "Will a day or two be sufficient?"

"One day," said B'oremos. "For it will take all of that for the court to come and view her."

I dared breath again. "As you will." And bowed. The peculiar thing is that I believed him. I was convinced that he and the court wanted to pay their respects to our dead Queen and it would never have occurred to any of them that we had tricked them. Though the princes might scheme, such Earth trickeries were beyond their imagining, or so it seemed to me. What a Queen says is true, and Dr. Z had been—in B'oremos's eyes—our Queen. But still, as Hopfner said, we didn't want to take any extra chances.

Dr. Z lay in state all that day with Hopfner standing at attention at her head, Clark at her feet, and a guard on either side. Whenever there was a break in the line of mourners, Hopfner complained to me.

"They are greatly honoring her," I said. "Normally, the dead body is shoved up onto a pyre for the birds. Only Queens are viewed and mourned." So he was stilled.

N'Jymnbo knelt frequently at Dr. Z's side, as if crying over her. In reality he was checking on the vital signs. Any change would be an indication of actual acute distress rather than transsleep, which would mean Plan B, or as Dr. Z had put it the night before, "which means getting me the bleep out of there. I'm not really a martyr type. Just a conscripted fairy tale motif."

As the last rays of the L'Lal'lorian sun were descending, and the gray fingers of night crept around our clearing, the Queen herself showed up, flanked by Linni and the priestess carrying the orb and rood.

The Queen sobbed, pronouncing the words that began the period of a Royal Seven: "A Queen has died. Let the tears flow." Then she left for the Hall of Grief, signaling us all to follow.

We left Hopfner, Clark, and N'Jymnbo on guard duty. I explained this small break in their ceremony in terms of the medieval concept of vigil (*Analogue, analogue*, I heard Dr. Z's voice in my mind), and though it was strange to B'oremos, it seemed likely. He did not insist that those three leave her side, though he left one of his own retainers, Mar-keshan, as a sign of further respect.

The Hall was lit by torches that flared upward toward the open roof. Though the mourners walked slowly to the sound of great pounding funerary drums, the shadows on the walls danced madly, creating an orgiastic parody of the somber procession. Only I seemed disturbed by the irony.

The L'Lal'lorians seemed really moved by Dr. Z's death, though they had known her only a day. We sky-farers reacted more like tourists than like grieving friends. I only hoped the Queen and her retinue would take such gawping as our traditional show of grief.

Linni mounted to the stage and, after her, B'oremos. They proceeded to speak and sing long throbbing dirgelike songs and sonorous poems backed by chordings of incredible minor progressions. This was grieving for a queen.

It was while Linni was chanting the third long poem of the night, and the crowds of mourners stood gazing raptly up at the stage, arms around one another, swaying to the rhythms of her words, that I began to realize what a truly great artist she was. For as I attended, with the years of training of a professional listener, I understood that she had woven in the few details of Dr. Z's life that she had been able to glean, adding observations of a physical nature that astounded me. And she did it all *as* she spoke within the strict confines of the rhyme scheme—intricate, formal, contrapuntal—and within an elongated metaphor of grief. It was a masterful performance.

The Queen standing near me sobbed openly, with little passionate gasps. She touched my hand and her fingers seemed to burn their prints onto my skin.

"I liked her," she said. "And I would have liked to know her more."

Biting back a quick answer about "Then why did you have her die?" I said instead, "She had already grown by your friendship. Had she known you longer, she would have grown more." Some imp inside me, with Dr. Z's voice, added, "Though some would say she had already grown quite enough."

"What did you say, A'ron, in that rough tongue of yours?" the Queen asked, and I realized with a start that I had spoken the last aloud in English.

"I said . . . may she grow in the Light," thinking again that light was something Dr. Z never was.

"Then you know of the Light, too," said the Queen. "We must talk of it. Come to my room now, that we may converse further." Her hand burned on mine.

"It is our custom to mourn by the side of our grieven one," I said, explaining "vigil" to her.

She looked at me through hooded eyes and left in a swirl of shadows, her servants following quickly.

I don't think I began to breath again until she was gone. Her hand's fire still burned atop mine long after she had left.

When the Queen had departed, the mourning ritual began to wind down slowly and at last Linni left the stage. Walking in a slow, cadenced manner to the beat of the drums, she marched over to me.

"Man Without Tears," she said, "I will grieve for you and yours not because the Queen commands it but because I sense that whatever else you tell the Queen, you do not—perhaps cannot—truly grieve."

"Perhaps I do not know how, Lina-Lania," I said.

"Perhaps there is no need," she answered.

I was stunned for a moment, wondering if she had seen through our charade. Then I decided that she was talking metaphorically about our lives in general as she perceived them.

"When there is neither plukenna nor ladanna but only an in-between state . . ." she began.

"Love is not in between," I said, "but better than both."

"That I do not believe."

"Perhaps you cannot."

"Perhaps there is no need."

It was not an argument but an antiphony and my heart beat with the rhythm of it. Her eyes were bright and, in the darkening Hall, seemed to glow.

Just then B'oremos joined us. "Thus ends the first night of mourning," he said. "We must feast, now, eating the portion which would ordinarily have gone to your Queen."

I smiled. "Then we will have much to eat."

Linni looked scandalized, but B'oremos clapped me on the back and though he did not laugh, I believe he came very close to it.

"Come back to my apartment. There will be plenty of good food. Mar-keshan prepared it early. Gray will come, too."

"Gray?"

"Lina-Lania. The Gray Wanderer. It is what we call her."

"Gray." I rolled it in my mouth, not quite liking the sound or implication.

Linni saw my hesitation. "Which name do you prefer?"

"Linni. It reminds me of the linnet, a little singing bird of Earth, my world."

"And what is the color of that bird?" she asked.

I smiled. "There *is* one variation called a gray linnet," I said.

"There," she said. "Words of two worlds cannot lie. Call me what you will."

"Linni," I said. "I will leave you *Gray* in B'oremos's mouth. For in our world that is a color that is somber, washed out, sad, without sparkle. It does not suit you."

"You do not, in fact, know what suits me yet, Man Without Tears," said Linni. "I sense that hesitation in you. A wondering and a holding back. A poem not yet sung."

I smiled directly at her, closing B'oremos out. "I will sing that poem someday, I promise you."

B'oremos insinuated himself back between us. Taking my right hand he pulled me out of the Hall of Grief across the cobbled streets to the palace, then through the maze of hallways to his rooms. Linni followed.

Did the Queen know that you had gone with them instead of back to the ship for your vigil?

I didn't know, nor, I must admit, did I give it any thought at the time. I told myself I was observing, studying, learning; a true anthro. But I think, in fact, I was enjoying.

Ladanna.

I beg your pardon, sir?

I was just musing. Carry on, Aaron.

In B'oremos's room I sank back against a fall of cushions as easily as if I had done so all my life. B'oremos lay back on his own, his foot touching against mine. Only Linni sat upright, like a punctuation mark between us.

I asked questions, phrased more like statements and B'oremos gave me answers phrased more like puzzles. It was almost a game between us and I was beginning to fit into their way of thinking. Just as there is a moment in the learning of a language when one suddenly dreams in the new tongue and knows it, so there is this moment of acculturation. We are told *of* it in the classroom, but the explanation is lame. When it comes, though, there is no mistaking it.

I had quite forgotten Dr. Z's "death," and so, when a servant arrived summoning B'oremos to the Queen's Apartment, I was unprepared for his heavy sigh.

"Grief makes her think of her immortalities," he said.

"Grief?" I asked. "Immortalities?" The long day and the glasses of wine that B'oremos served, much stronger than any I had yet tried, were making me slow.

"The death of your Queen grieves her and she thinks of the time when she, herself a Queen, will be in the Cave without the comfort of blood daugh-

ters to mourn her. She longs for another child. Tonight she insists on being sown and we will all be
rewarded if there is a harvest."

"She asked me," I said. "She invited me to her
room but I told her no."

B'oremos and Linni looked shocked.

"One does not deny a Queen," Linni said.

"We do our sowing with *love*," I said. "And with
love there is always a choice."

"A man has no choice in these matters," said
B'oremos. "A man has so little time, it must be
expended in the service of the Queen. She calls and
I . . ." He brushed his hand across the front of his
chiton and there was a noticeable bulge there. "I
am a man and must answer." He looked at me
grimly. "Either you are playing with us and are not
a man or—"

"I am a man," I said simply.

"Or for you time runs at a different pace," Linni
finished.

To this I made no answer. I did not dare.

B'oremos touched my shoulder and left quickly
by a door that was hidden behind a drapery, and
Linni and I were left alone.

"*Is* time different for you?" she asked.

I tried to think of a way to phrase it so that it
would not further compromise our mission. "We
count in a different way," I said at last.

She was silent for a while, her angular face solemn, reminding me of madonnas on the glass windows of cathedrals on old Earth. Finally she looked
at me. "You have much to teach us, sky-farer."

"I am here to learn, not to teach," I said, my
mind strangely sharp. I seemed to see each word
before pronouncing it. Absently, I reached out to

pluck a word out of the air, turned it over in my
hand, and said, "The word is *ladanna*."

"I will teach you the difference between plukenna and ladanna," said Linni, "without words."
She said it earnestly. "For it is certain I cannot
teach a man to grieve unless he feels that grief
here." She moved over to sit close to me and
touched me over the heart, her hand palm down,
fingers spread wide.

"But where does a man feel the difference between plukenna and ladanna if not here?" I said,
covering her hand with mine. Hers trembled beneath.

"I have never been *touched*," she answered,
then added as if the simple statement needed explaining. "In my village I was odd, even odder than
the usual Royal sowing. And here, as I am the
Queen's Own Griever, I am Untouchable. Do you
understand what that means?"

"Little linnet," I said, almost whispering,
"sweet singer. I, too, have never been *touched*. I've
been too busy studying and learning. But now—it
would also be against all my vows to touch you."

Her hand moved off my heart and onto my lips.

I kissed her fingers one by one. They were rough-
ened and there was a crescent-shaped scar on her
left thumb. Then I dropped her hand and reached
for my cup of wine and drained it. On the bottom
lay a single small black seed like a period at the end
of a sentence.

"What is this?" I asked.

She took the cup and looked, then put her hand
to her brow. "It is what is left of a Lumin nut after
it has been soaked in wine. B'oremos had those
three Kernels which your Dot'der'tsee gave back

to him. He has put one in the cup for you."

"Oh, God. Am I a dead man?" I asked, beginning to feel a warmth swelling up my legs. If this was death, it was not at all unpleasant.

"Oh, no, A'ron, not dead. Three kernels bring death. Two will give you nightmares and hysteria. But one . . ." Her voice became soft and out of focus. "One is for a night of wild rejoicing."

"Have you, too, drunk wine with a kernel?" I asked, suddenly eager for her answer.

She looked into her cup, drained it, looked again. Her eyes were golden and wide. "We will be unable to stop what has already begun," she said. "If there is a fault, if there has been a betrayal, it is B'ore-mos's. You—and I—we are innocent." She rose, blew out the candles one by one by one, then came toward me in the lingering shadows and lay down by my side.

The first kiss and the first touch were sweet, but not as sweet as all the ones that followed.

You need not describe any more, Aaron.

Thank you, sir, but I could not even if ordered. The Lumin muddled my senses and I'm not sure what was real and what was not. But I love her, sir. And I know she loves me.

What makes you say that?

Because as she was blowing the candles out, I looked into her cup. There was no little black seed in it.

Ladies and gentlemen, you have all heard Aaron Spenser's testimony. I want you to consider it carefully. There are three things to examine: motive for contamination, method of contamination, and of course whether in fact contamination has occurred.

Excuse me, sir, but there is something that I don't understand. What happened between Linni and me was personal. When B'oremos returned, Linni and I had already parted, she to her own room and I back to the ship, where I was to help prepare Dr. Z's transfer into a transsleep capsule. Linni and I had decided that we needed time to sort through our feelings about what had happened, though we were not going to speak of it to anyone else. She reminded me that vows broken under the influence of Lumin do not count. So I have been puzzled all along at this Court Martial. But as I promised to tell the truth of it to this court, I have—to the best of my ability.

However, that day, without warning, I was sent up here, ostensibly to accompany the casket, which, as medical officer of the landing party, N'Jymnbo should have done. And I have been up here over twenty days, not being allowed to contact Linni. I've been given makework—translations of some tapes, chordings of grief songs. But no one will tell me what is happening on planetfall, sir. Even Dr. Z avoids me. I admit a certain amount of cultural contamination happened, but—as I tried to explain— there were circumstances.

Aaron, *circumstances* have changed. Greatly. This morning Dr. N'Jymnbo flew up with a present from the Queen.

A present, sir?

A seven-pound squalling present, Aaron. Blond, too, which is something never seen before on L'Lal'lor, though she has their golden eyes. Your twenty days labtime has been almost a full year down below, you know.

A girl *baby*, sir?

Yes, Aaron.

And what of Linni?

From what we understand, she believes the child was a boy and born dead. And as you know, if the Queen herself had not offered the child to us, we would have had to take her anyway. She is a living contamination there. Here she is simply a beautiful, healthy baby, a citizen of the Federation.

May I—may I see my child, sir?

See her? Aaron, if you are found guilty, as I fully expect you to be, you will have the job of raising her.

Thank you, sir.

Should I reread the charge, Captain Macdonald?
Do so, Lieutenant.

Aaron Spenser, the charge is Cultural Contamination as defined by the USS Code #27. The specification is that you willfully and unlawfully violated the Cultural Contact Contamination Act in regards to your relationship with an inhabitant or inhabitants of the planet Henderson's IV, thus influencing—to the good or to the bad—all culture within their closed system forever.

Ladies and gentlemen, the vote is yours. In the case of a tie, I shall be forced to cast the deciding vote. Consider carefully.

Court Martial Inquiry dismissed.
We will meet back here in 0800 hours.

Sir, we have voted.
What say you to the charge, Yeoman Peterson?

Guilty, sir, with extenuating circumstances.
"Circumstances" is a word that seems to pop up with surprising regularity in these proceedings.

Begging your pardon, sir, but the proper form—

Form, schmorm, as my great-grandmother used to say. Ladies and gentlemen, what recommendation for sentence?

Five years' work aboard space lab, sir, including child-rearing. No further contact during that period with Henderson's IV or any of its inhabitants.

Excuse me, sir. But . . .

Is there something wrong with the form now, Lieutenant?

I just thought that you might like to add that, at the end of that time, the words Court Martial Sentence *be deleted from Anthro First Class Spenser's records. Because of the extenuating circumstances, sir. It's permitted, sir, in Article 763 of the Court Martial Code.*

Why, Lieutenant, a heart beats beneath that iron exterior.

It's . . . um . . . regulation issue at the Academy, sir.

A joke, too. I'm beginning to like you, Lieutenant. And I would like to do that, add that. Use the proper numbers and article references.

Yes, sir.

Any last words before I dismiss us all, Aaron?

What about Linni, sir?

That, my boy, is up to her—and her people. I suspect, though, that she will be forgiven if she is anywhere near the artist you say she is. Whether she, herself, will forgive—that is beyond my guessing.

Then, sir, I'd like to see my child.

Tape 9:

QUEEN OF SHADOWS

Place: _Queen's Throne Room_
Time: _Queen's Time 76, Thirteenth Matriarchy, lahtime 2137.5 A.D._
Speaker: _Queen to Aaron Spenser_
Permission: _Queen's own_

A Queen does not tell stories. She tells the truth. Even her lies are true. That is the prerogative of Royalty. So what I am about to tell you is, of course, true. What you choose to believe, seeing that you are neither a Royal nor of our world, is your own concern. But know this, man from the sky, I am the Queen and I speak true.

Only a Queen can bear Queens and since a Queen speaks the truth, whomever she designates as the father of her children is so. If you do not understand this about our world, you understand nothing.

We grieve for our dead and dying in a way that makes the passage beautiful and gives the grieven one immortality. So our greatest grievers, the ones who bring many mourners into the lines, who give us life after death, are the ones we cherish the most. We do many things for them, things that may appear not true but become true with the telling. If I choose to name Lina-Lania my child and you the father, it will be so. Oh, do not look so worried, A'ron. I am past such namings now. I am tired, burned away. There is little time left for me, now, so I would tell you—of all people—why. And is that not why you are here? To find out why. Why I did what I did to the Gray Wanderer, the greatest of all our grievers, and my favorite. Why I took her from you. Why I told her truths which she could not accept and yet, by accepting them as she was bound to do, betrayed you forever.

We are both older now, though you do not look as if more than a year or two has passed. And I, like all Queens, have not changed either. It is a strange mortality we women of the Royals have. We do not age until the day we die and then, in a moment, we turn into a dried-out husk, ashes inside, ready for the pylons. I saw my mother and my sisters transformed that way, in seconds their beauty gray dust over bones. It is why our people view our husks—to see for themselves that we are indeed dust.

I see by your face that you do not believe this. Believe it. A Queen has told you so.

But as old as we are, A'ron, the Gray Wanderer is older still. Fifty years have passed since you spoke to her last, and those fifty years have been etched like poems onto her face. Her hands are writ with the calligraphy of time. Those are her metaphors, not mine. She gives everything to me. I am her Queen.

It was prophesied that she would be the child to lead us, that she would be betrayed but would forgive the betrayal. And that is why I have chosen you, now, to learn the truth, or at least as much of the truth as a Queen will tell. Believe it or not. Believe what you will or what you can. You have my permission to write it down, though we know that only what is held in the mouth is true.

And you may tell all this to your own Queen, for I know that she never died but lives on despite her death, which makes her a greater Queen than I, an inheritor of a stranger immortality. I know this because, like all Queens, I have my spies. And some of them are liars and some of them are not. But I know that this thing is true, for she did not dry up as a Queen must, but died and lived in her glass box.

Come then, sit by me with your back against this black cushion, which my favorites have used for so many years. See, it is embroidered with the great red creature your own Queen favored. I have placed it close to me always, that her immortality may touch my own. The Gray Wanderer often lay there, occupying that same place, her back where your back now rests. She occupied it—but we never touched. Touching would have been a violation of her vows, and how could she, then, grieve for me when I die?

And now she lives in a cave far up in the hills and thinks I know not where she stays. She can see the palace from that hill, but I can see the hill from the twin towers, so what is there between us but air?

She will not talk to me, she says, because I tryst with men from the sky. She says their *love* is cold and barren and a lie. But I know better and I know, too, that when it is time she will come and grieve for me because she has never revoked her vows. She is a griever. She is the Queen's Own Griever.

What cave? Where?

Do not rush away, seeking her. Not yet, A'ron. What you find in that cave is not what you expect. Listen to my story first. Trust the truth of it and then I will give you leave to go.

We will sit here, just the two of us, until the fingers of the shadow world reach into ours and the tale is done.

I like this time, the cusp of day, when the world sits between light and dark. It makes me remember. Queens have long memories, A'ron, and I like to indulge mine.

Do you not fear my anger?

Time does not hone anger, A'ron. It blunts it. What you have is not anger but a long sorrow. A grief. We are a people who understand grief. I am not afraid of you. Are you afraid of me?

I do not understand.

Your Linni is changed beyond loving. She is now an old, old woman. But you and I have aged little. Once you ran from my bed in fear, now you will run from hers. I have no interest in you now. Though your face is still such a pretty one, it is too broad between the eyes for my liking. I prefer my boys simpler and fifty years—or five—is a long time to set a preference.

So you know about the time changes.

A Queen knows everything. I know past and present and future. I see so clearly I see the shadows. Do you know that I am called Queen of Shadows?

I have heard it.

And why do you think I am so called?

Perhaps because you sit in a darkening room like an old lace-foot spinning shadow webs of deceit.

Not, that would be too poetic. Grievers think that way. I am not a metaphor, I am a Queen. But of course this room that I keep dark feeds the rumors and keeps the name alive. Still, that is not why I am so called.

Some say it is because I am the last of the Queens. Barren. My womb empty as a cave on the hill. My children only passing shades. And my brothers and nephews sow weakly. Even their girl children age. They are not Royal.

So it is true that I rule in a time of shadows. As we are shadowed by the great ships that brought you here to change all our lives.

We did not try to change your lives. We have tried to be most careful of that.

You are here, A'ron. That very fact brings changes. So my people become their own shadows under the tutors from the stars.

But that is still not why I am called Queen of Shadows. It is because of the story I told, the un-truth that I made true to hold on to the one I loved above all others, the Gray Wanderer. She believed me, knowing all the while that what I told her was untrue. I did it because she was so dear to me, with-out searching out what would serve our world best. And that lie come true has condemned our world. I know that there is no saving us. We are changed beyond all recognition. I am the shadow Queen in truth, like the mad Queen of the tale after whom I am named. She who so desired a reflection of her-self—for that is what grievers are, you know: pools that reflect. Once I thought they reflected clearly, but it is not so. The old mad Queen desired her own image, forsaking the one she *should* have desired, and so gave away her kingdom's treasure. Oh, that is a story I could tell.

Give me your hand now. My touch will no longer sear it. You see, you *are* beginning to age, sky-farer. Is my hand so? One of your own, the tall hard one called Hop'nor. He told me that it is believed by

some of your world that the lines of our hands could
be read as one reads a map, the goings and comings
traced so. But when I asked him to read mine he
could not, for my hands have no lines on them at
all. See? That is because a Queen writes her own
history and that history can be read only by the
Queen herself.

Tell me of Linni and the cave.

You who have so much time cannot bear to
lengthen it. Very well, then, listen. It is—and is
not—by way of a confession.

When you excused yourself from my bed with
the unkindest of excuses, I knew it to be a lie. But
no one lies to a Queen. So the paradox began, the
unraveling of the skein that binds up this world.

I had you followed. What Queen does not have
such shadows at her command? I knew that you
went into the rooms of B'oremos, where you and
he lay, drinking wine. He was still young, with the
taste of his boyhood friends still fresh and a passion
for the odd, the different, the prodigy, as he was
himself odd, different, a prodigy. I did not want him
to have what I did not. So I summoned him to me,
out of anger, out of jealousy, out of desire. And he
came, afire with Lumin-laced wine, hard and eager
and full of seed. I thought certainly I would reap a
child. But in the morning, when the Lumin wore off
and he knew me, he told me there were kernels in
three cups: one for him, one for you, and then he
smiled and said that there had been one for the Gray
Wanderer, too. He had no shame of the act. His
shame was that he had not been there to complete
it. I could have struck him, but I did not, for I realized that if I had no girl children, he would make
a fine King, devious and truthful at one and the same
time. So I called him my heir over all others. But I

sent him from me at that moment as a lesson in Queenship, telling him there was one more thing he had to do before his night's work was over.

"And that is?" he dared to ask.

"Go to the silver tower on the plain and tell them that their A'ron has abused my friendship and violated my person and that I will send him away or kill him."

His face was angry, stunned, but I was the Queen. So he went to the ship and Hop'nor came down the stairs and believed all that he was told.

B'oremos returned and asked me what would befall now.

I said that you would be sent away with your dead Queen to be punished or not by your own people. And he listened and believed and it was so.

What did you tell Linni?

I told her that what she thought she had done was all a dream sent by the Lumin and not true. That her vows had not been violated. I told her that your dreams had driven you away. That men from the skies were full of deceit and honeyed words, but they did not know the difference between what is true and what is a lie.

She looked at me and said, "Was it not prophesied that I will forgive all betrayals?" Then she bowed her head and was gone.

Then how did you explain the child to her?

Explain what child, A'ron?

Oh, come now, the child that was born. Golden-haired and golden-eyed.

But I just explained, A'ron. There could have been no child between the two of you because there was no touching. There was no touching because of her vows. How, therefore, could there be a child? It was all a Lumin dream.

There was no Lumin in her cup. I saw it. It was empty. B'oremos lied to you.

Man Without Tears, *you* lie.

It is true I am capable of lying. But now I tell you the truth.

Ah, but then you must see that if she knew, she chose not to know because her Queen told her so.

She was brought to childbed in the cave but never made a sound. B'oremos attended her. He said she made not even the smallest mewling.

Perhaps he fed her the last Lumin nut.

If that last one is not a lie.

If it is, it is not my lie.

B'oremos took the child away. Only he and I know of it. It was a strange child. I held it and touched its yellow hair. Then I gave it to him to bring to the tower. Hop'nor thought it was our child, yours and mine. I almost kept her. If her hair had been dark, I would have. But then Gray would have known.

She is a beautiful child. And she never cries.

Still alive, then? I am glad.

But you sent her away.

The Gray Wanderer was untouched. That is the truth, for the Queen has spoken it.

Then the Queen lies. My daughter—and Linni's—lives. She is a bright, golden-haired girl of five. She already reads and writes and has a great gift—of laughter.

I do not lie, A'ron; I choose well. For it is clear to me now that *this* is the child of whom the prophesy speaks. Fifty years ago our world was not ready for the way in which she would lead. I only hope it is, now.

May I see Linni?

Do you think she would want to have you see her as an old woman? She may have too much pride for that.

Do you worry about her pride, my lady, or do you worry more that she will hate you for what you have done?

One cannot hate a Queen. And the Gray Wanderer will mourn for me whether she wishes to or not. She is, after all, the Queen's Own Griever and she will bring many mourners to my lines. For I am the last of the Queens and when she grieves for me, she grieves for an entire civilization. B'oremos will be a strong King, but whether he will be a wise one I do not know.

Were you strong? Were you wise?

I was the last. That is enough. Come, hand me that Cup. I would drink of it.

First tell me of the cave.

You do not trust me yet, A'ron.

Trust you? I have learned too much about you in the intervening years. I know also that, having confessed to me, you would involve me in your death by having me hand you the Cup of Sleep.

And you are unwilling?

Oh, I am willing enough. Not because I wish you dead, but because I wish your culture alive and that means following your rituals out to the end. But first speak to me of the cave.

It is north of here, but still within sight of the city. There is a pathway of sorts. B'oremos will take you. He has been listening to our conversation. That drapery hides not a wall but a niche. He knows what to do. He is my own true son in this, though often I had wished him a girl.

Then here is the Cup of Sleep.

You will make them remember me?

My lady, you will be remembered on two worlds.
May your lines of mourning be long.

May your time of dying be . . . My God.

She did not lie to you. About the ashes. It is
not a pretty sight.

Then you are now King, B'oremos.

I will have the servants put that *thing* out on
the pylons. The people will have days of good
viewing.

But she was your Queen.

She is now no more than a Thing. And besides,
she made me lie three times to Gray. Now I am
King and what *I* say is true. I will bring Gray back
from the hills.

Thank you, B'oremos.

I bring her back for me—not for you. Still you
do not understand, A'ron. She is the best griever
after all. The King's Own Griever. There is need
of her now.

God, you're a cold bastard.

No, I am not cold. That was a mistake *she*
made. I burn. Burn. And I have a longer memory
than the Queen could ever know. Time does not
blunt anger, A'ron. It takes the sharp edge and
hones it to a killing point. Now I am King and I
may strike as I will.

Will you strike me?

No, but I will tell you what really happened,
that you may better know what it is you do and
have done here. If that is a blow, then you—not
I—have struck it.

And Linni?

She will do what she has always done best.
Grieve.

Tape 10:

CHILD OF EARTH
AND SKY

Place: *Palace of the King, Apartment of the King*

Time: *King's Time 1, First Patriarchy; labtime 2137.5+ A.D.*

Speaker: *The King, called B'oremos, also called the Singer of Dirges, to Aaron Spenser*

Permission: *King's own*

She was mad, of course. All Queens are mad. Mad with grief; mad with the touching; mad with power. It is the one final prerogative of Royalty. I, too, perhaps am mad. But my madness is tempered by the long patience of princes. After the five years of sowing seed, we no longer serve but we wait.

I *loved* you, you know. Perhaps I am the only one of this planet of grievers who truly understands that word. It does not mean desire. The Queen's summons brings desire. A Lands girl's payment is desire. Even the touch of prince to prince is desire. But I *loved* you. I saw in you my other self, my golden half. And Gray was the shadow between us.

So when the Queen bade me come to her, fresh from your side, I gave her all my desire and my seed, but I thought of you maddened by the Lumin, waiting for me. I never expected Gray, to whom I had given no such wine, to stay.

But I returned at dawn and the two of you lay, tangled together amongst my cushions. You were in the deep, full sleep of Lumin. But she was restless, and under her eyelids the amber eyes were

155

roaming as if seeking a place of peace. Even in her sleep she remembered the violation of her vows. I hated her then even as I had desired her. I wanted to hurt her in such a way that you would be hurt, too. My prince's mind plotted well.

I returned to the Queen and lied.

It is not an easy thing to lie to a Queen. But having met you, A'ron, I was not the silly young boy I had been. Your arrival made me a man. I saw what men *could* do. And so I lied.

"I am not the only one who has joyed tonight," I said to her.

She preened herself, thinking I had returned for her. "I, too, B'oremos. It was a night of wild sowing. There will be many children born."

"There may be many children, O Queen, but they will not spring from between your legs. Nor will they come from mine."

She looked puzzled. "Do you prophesy, princeling? But then you must shave your head."

"Even a prince can read this orb," I said. "In my room lie two who drank of the Lumin and, forgetting vows, made a child."

She stood in a fury. I had never seen her so. Her hair crackled with little fires. Her eyes turned nearly black. "Gray?" she croaked. "You dared feed Lumin to her?"

I smiled.

She reached up and smoothed down her hair and calmed the rage somewhat. "But a vow broken by Lumin is not a vow broken."

"Gray is not what she was."

"Gray is still Gray. She is my Master Griever. Nothing happened. The Queen speaks true."

She was magnificent, A'ron. She was the Queen. She sat back down amidst her cushions, running a

finger across her upper lip, a sure sign that she was
thinking. Then she smiled up at me and patted a
place by her side. I sat.

"You have no shame," she murmured, her hands
loosening my bindings, her voice stirring the Lumin-
heightened senses again, "I like that in a prince."
And she fell upon me and in that position I once
again sowed my Queen.

When she raised herself from me, she said, "But
your night's work is not yet over."

I could barely move. I told her so.

She touched me fiercely with her nails and I cried
out. "This," she said, "this is nothing. And soon
you shall be nothing, while I live on to be plowed
and plowed again. Still I have a task for you, my
princeling."

"And that is . . ."

"Go to the silver tower on the plain. Find the tall
one. The old one with the beard. I suspect he still
stores his seed, unlike you, my little prince, who
will soon be able to sow only plots and intrigues.
Tell him . . . tell him his A'ron has abused my
friendship and violated my person. This way!" She
ripped her nails across her breast, leaving red lines.
"And this!" She clawed at her thighs until they bled.
"Tell them that he dared sow a Queen against her
will."

"Who will believe that?" I asked.

"They will believe. A Queen does not lie."

I nodded.

"Tell them to take him away or I will have him
killed."

So I went at once to the ship, first ordering Mar-
keshan to wake the two of you and get the Gray
Wanderer home. Hop'nor believed what he was told
because the Queen said it. And when he saw her

wounds, he knelt down and kissed her hand and spoke softly to her, which she enjoyed. Then he and his companions took you into the ship and we did not see you again until this day.

But it was all lies. So many lies.

And yet it was all true.

Because the Queen made it so?

Because it *was* so. What happens is only a shadow of what is, A'ron.

What did you say to Linni?

I told her that the lords of the air and sky are full of deceits. I told her that you were a betrayer. But she stopped me with her hand upon my mouth, a kind of pitying touch she should not have given.

She said, "The Queen has told me all, but I forgive all, *all* betrayers, B'oremos, my only friend."

Then she went out to lead the grieving for your dead Queen.

I suppose you wonder as well about the birth of the child, the child of earth and sky.

I wonder.

It was—and was not—like any birth. It began with joy and ended with tears. There were many years of grieving.

That is not enough.

And if I tell you all, golden A'ron, will you, like Gray, forgive the betrayals?

I have the child, B'oremos. I can forgive.

Then listen well, for there are things here that no one else but you and I will know.

When Gray was but three months gone with child, three people knew of it.

You, the Queen—and Gray.

How little you understand the heart, A'ron, for all that you study us. The three you named were the three who would not let themselves know, who denied what was true.

The three who knew the shadows behind the Queen's truth were these: T'arremos, my map-scarred enemy; D'oremos, my mentor; and the man of Waters I held closest to me, Mar-keshan.

They guessed what they did not know and named me sower, violator. T'arremos told D'oremos in order to curry favor. Mar-keshan told D'oremos in order to save me. But D'oremos went to the Queen because it needed to be said.

The Queen swore it was untrue and D'oremos had to believe her. D'oremos swore it was untrue, and T'arremos chose not to believe him. Mar-keshan knew what was, *was*; he came to me.

Bowing low, he spoke in that soft burring voice that reminded me of the sea itself. "I have something to tell you, lord, as a friend. Will you walk into the courtyard with me?"

And he added with his fingers rapidly, "It is the Gray."

I went.

And there, away from prying ears to hear us and prying eyes to read our hands, he told me what he suspected and I, trusting him, told him what was true.

He went at once to Gray's rooms because a servant can come and go quietly and no one remarks him. And late that night two servants—an old man from Waters and a stooped-over old woman from Lands (grief paints can make many changes in a face) left for a cave high up in the hills.

The Queen said her Own Griever was ill and had gone home to her people. And because the Queen so said it, it was true. And she said that T'arremos was in great pain and had taken the Cup, which was surprising for one so young, but not out of the question since the mark on his face had been a sign of inner sickness.

That was true—and it was not true.

What about it was true?

That he died.

And what was not true?

I killed him. With my hands. For he came into my apartment after Gray had left, and he spit at me and smirked with that twisted mouth of his and called me a betrayer. I had been thinking about betrayals before he had arrived, and it was as if a great red fog came over me. When it lifted, T'arremos was beneath me. I was astraddle him and his neck was in my hands. But there was no breath left in his body and his face was a grayish-blue, the map on it near purple. I let him drop and ran to D'oremos, who took me in without a word and listened and sighed. He bade me wait while he spoke with the Queen. And without a summons, which was daring on his part, he went to her.

When he returned, he had the Queen's Own Cup in his hands.

"Put this by his body on your cushions. Then return here. Spend the night with me and I will teach you of other pleasures the Queen does not know. We will let someone else find T'arremos. It will be said that he took the Cup, because you would not touch him, but that what was twisted in him allowed him no quick or easy death. Then we will grieve him briefly as befits a prince, but without great ceremony as is due an unbeliever. For he did not believe the Queen's truth and so he deserved to die."

I did as D'oremos advised, and when I returned
he had fruits and wines set out for us and we spent
a long and joyous night. In that way he bound me
to him, with bonds even tighter than before, but he
was a fine adviser and I learned much of Queenship
from him over the years.

But the birth?

Yes, the birth. You want to know of birth, not
death. But they are so intertwined. Patience, A'ron,
is the prerogative—

*Of Royalty. Yes, I know. Everything is the pre-
rogative of Royalty. Just tell me of the birth.*

For five more months Gray lived in the cave
tended by Mar-keshan. And once a week I went
riding in the hills on the Queen's white horse, smelling the windstrife and picking trillis. I brought a sad-
dlebag of fruits and sweets and other things to tempt
Gray's appetite, though she wanted nothing but the
food that Mar-keshan gathered for her. He had
tamed a wild she-goat for the milk. They lived like
father and daughter, if you can imagine it.

I can imagine it.

And then one day when I was there, her pains
began and so I stayed. She did not cry out, not once,
though I saw the passage of the child inside ripple
her belly like waves upon the sea.

"Do you know what to do, Mar-keshan?" I
asked, suddenly afraid.

"I am a man of Waters," he said. "And children
come out riding a wave. Do not fear, my lord."

So I stopped being afraid. Instead I mixed up a
potion of wine and a single Lumin, the one left over,
the one I had never given Gray, the one I kept with
me in a silken purse strung 'round my neck.

"Drink," I said to her during the quiet time between waves. "This will soothe the passage."

So, trusting me, she drank. And when she started
to fade, she forgave me again with her eyes.

The child was born and she never woke to see it.
It came, as Mar-keshan said, riding a wave. Its skin
was blue until Mar-keshan hit its back with his palm.
Then it cried and turned pink and white. And when
he cleaned it of its strange frothy covering, I saw
what I had feared. The babe was a girl and she had
golden hair.

"Then you must take her," Mar-keshan said.

I nodded. He had been with me so long, he knew
my mind.

"What will you tell Gray?"

Mar-keshan did not hesitate. "When she wakes,
I will tell her that she had a boy child and it was
born dead and that all this happened days ago and
the body is long broken apart on the pyre. She will
accept it."

"Queen's truth," I said.

"Queen's truth," he answered, but there were
tears of grief in his eyes. "She is a beautiful child."

But whether he meant the child I bore in my arms
or the one who slept lulled by Lumin in the straw,
I did not know.

And . . .

I brought the child back and into the palace by
the secret way. The Queen held her for a moment
and touched her yellow hair, then gave her to me.

"Tell them the child is mine and that I want none
of her."

So I did. And you know the rest.

Tape 11:

TRANSMISSION TO COMMAND

Place: Cave #27
Time: King's Time 1, First Patriarchy; labtime 2137.5 + A.D.
Speaker: Aaron Spenser to Captain James Macdonald, USS Venture
Permission: Directed transmission

Sir, I am presuming that you will hear this, as I know this cave, which you call Cave #27 and we call home, is under preset voice-activated status. I am alone now, which is why I am able to speak this way. The women are out and I pled a small fever, which is somewhat true. So they have left me to pick some healing berries for a tisane.

I want to set the record straight. I have not *gone native* in the old sense. And I have not—Dr. Z, please note— gone against the teachings of Anthro Guild. I will not bring to my people anything beyond their own discovering or change their essential character. And please tell Dr. Z I remember the three things she warned me about. First, I am not being a romantic about the L'Lal'lorians but I *am* in love. Second, I hope I am no longer the adolescent twit she accused me of being. I think this whole experience has caused me to grow up. And third, this *is* my job: raising my child, loving my woman, fitting into my adopted world.

You must already know that I brought my child down. I suspect Dr. Z discovered it first, since she is Linnet's godmother. But rest easy. Linnet thrives down here. She loves her two mothers and has already learned the language with that casual ease only a small child can achieve. I will not let her forget Standard English, though, that I promise you. She is, after all, the child who is to lead the way, and the way leads straight to the stars. It has already been prophesied, you know, so this is no kind of contamination.

When B'oremos and I first rode up to the cave, I didn't know what to expect. I had been told Linni was old and I knew that because of the Hulanlocke Rotational Device the five years I had spent in the lab had been fifty here. Yet there was a tall, handsome young woman standing outside the cave working on a scaffolding of branches. Her long, dark hair was caught up in a braided crown and she was frowning with the hard work.

"Linni!" I cried out to her before B'oremos could stop me.

She looked up and in that instant I knew I was mistaken. She had a slightly lower forehead and a wider mouth than Linni ever had, though she was beautiful in much the same way.

There was a movement by the cave's mouth and an old woman, leaning on a stick, moved forward into the light. Her hair was still as black as a young girl's and the gold of her eyes unmistakable, but her skin had darkened and cracked with a fine webbing of lines. She looked like a familiar painting dimmed and crackled with time.

I leaped from the steed and went over to her. I was terrified, I'll admit. Standing before her, I took

her hand in mine and put it, fingers outspread, palm
over my heart.

"You . . . have not aged," she said, her voice
still melodic and low.

"You . . ." I began, thinking to lie to her.

She placed her hand on my mouth. "Do not try
to make me believe what cannot be believed," she
said. "I am done with that."

"I have a long truth to tell you," I said. "It is
full of betrayals, but none of my own."

B'oremos shifted uneasily in his saddle.

"I am past betraying," Linni said, her eyes
brimmed about with tears. "Three times is enough
for any woman." She looked past me at B'oremos.

"There *was* a child," he said quickly. "But I did
only what the Queen ordered."

"I knew there was a child," said Linni, "for I
carried her under my heart. And for all that you told
me it was a boy, born twisted and dead, I did not
believe you, though it was the Queen herself who
ordered it believed."

"Then why . . . ?" B'oremos got down from his
mount and came to us. I turned slightly so that I
was side by side with her and we stood together
against him.

"Because before all, I am the Queen's Own
Griever," she said, "and the first betrayal was my
own."

I picked up her hand again, feeling the fine tra-
ceries of age like a raised map beneath my fingers.
"The child lives."

"Lives!" It was a breath, a respiration filled with
joy.

"She has lived these years up in the sky with me,
so she is but five years old."

"Tell me of her."

I paused. "She is a golden child. A child of earth and sky. She sings like a little bird and her name is Linnet. She is always happy."

"A child!" This time it was the dark-haired girl who spoke. "But Gray, you never told me, not in all this time."

Gray left my side and went to her and put her arms around her as a mother does with a beloved daughter. "I have and have not a child," she said. Then, as if making up her mind, she turned to me. "Would you bring the little one here?"

"She is already in the silver tower. I brought her down, though I did it secretly."

Gray turned back to the girl. "Listen well and hold these words in your mouth and heart, for there will be a time when you will have to say them to our people. For my sake, this child is yours. And for the child's sake, too."

The girl nodded silently, though not speaking cost her an effort.

"I would stay here with Linnet," I said. "I am her father."

B'oremos cleared his throat. "You will need the King's permission," he said.

"King?" the girl spoke sharply.

"The Queen is dead?" said Linni, softly.

"Yes."

"Then I must go and grieve for her."

"Gray, you are not well," the girl protested.

Linni stood tall and tossed away her stick. "I am the Queen's Own Griever. Take me to her."

B'oremos picked her up with great gentleness and put her onto his horse, leaped up behind her, and they rode off. My horse shied at their going and it was fully a minute before I could calm it down enough to mount it.

I extended my hand to the girl. "Are you coming?"

"What? To mourn that unfeeling, quarrelsome old woman?" she asked. "I'd sooner eat Lumin."

I laughed at her words and she had the grace to blush, but she did not recall them. In the end she came, riding behind me, not because the Queen needed mourners for her lines but because Gray needed someone to clothe her and wrap her ankles and rub her brow and brew her the tisanes that eased the aching in her bones. And because she was curious about the child.

The girl's name, I found out on that wild ride down the mountainside, was Grenna. She was a pig-keeper's only daughter with a wild talent for art and she was Linni's personal apprentice. "*I* am the Gray Wanderer's child," she said with bitter pride in her voice, as if challenging me to deny her. She was twenty-one with a strange, attractive voice that caught every once in a while like a rag on a nail, tearing. She was angry, courageous, loyal to a fault, tender, sharp-tongued, anarchic, and funny. In many ways she was a combination of us and L'Lal'lor. We had already changed her—and her contemporaries—in our own image, you see. We hadn't meant it to happen, it just did. But Grenna had lived with the Gray Wanderer and so there was much of the old ways built into her thinking as well. I couldn't help but love her—for who she was and who she was becoming, and because she seemed a bridge between Linni and me.

We picked up Linnet from the tower where she'd
been sleeping, a rag doll Dr. Z had made clutched
in her arms. Then we walked into the city. Grenna
let Linnet ride on her shoulders, which endeared
her to both of us at once. And that is how we entered
the Hall of Grief, a family already, mourners who
had no tears to shed for the dusty husk of a Queen.

Gray was on the stage, still in the coarse dress
she had been wearing in the cave. A young prince
sat at her feet, strumming a brightly colored plecta.
Gray's voice was smooth and strong, but the poems
she spoke about the Queen did not move me. The
boy's fingers stumbled several times. I noticed that
particularly because I was used to the tapes of the
young B'oremos playing the same tune. The plecta
the boy was using was a bit tinny in the higher reg-
isters and the drone string buzzed.

The mourners moved dutifully in long serpentine
lines that seemed to have no beginning and no end,
and the world mourned the full Seven for the last
of their Queens. And though I was not moved, I was
comforted by the familiarity, the rightness of it all.
I felt—no, I *knew* I had come home.

Linnet, of course, was bored by the second hour
in the Hall of Grief and I took her back to the palace,
where she ran happily through the mazed halls and
the fully flowered courtyards. Her golden hair, just
a shade darker than mine had been at that age,
seemed to gather in all the light of the L'Lal'lorian
day, and many were the servants who, after at-
tending the grieving, came to watch her play. I found
myself thinking that old Mar-keshan would have
loved her, the child who had come into his arms
riding a wave. If I was sad about anything in that

seven days of mourning, it was that he was not there to see her.

After the Seven, Gray helped crown B'oremos, but it was a quiet, even desultory, affair. No one had much heart for it. Gray was exhausted, even with Grenna's constant fussing over her. The priestess was totally confused by my appearance and overwhelmed by Linnet's. And B'oremos wanted the ceremony done as quickly as possible because, as he put it, "Such ceremony reminds us of change. I wish my people to remember only that Kings have always been."

So Gray, Grenna, Linnet, and I went back up to the cave, where I hoped we might all get to know one another. And we had a few short months of it, like a happy summer vacation. Linnet came to call Gray Mama One, and Grenna Mama Two. It was an idyll.

And then Gray died. It was not *un*expected, I suppose. She and Grenna had been building her pylon the day I had arrived. But *I* had not expected it, though I do not know what magic I had hoped for. I mourned for a very long time, my own kind of mourning. Grenna was surprised that I could shed tears. And Linnet mourned as a child does, tearful one minute, then suddenly laughing and dancing away to pick flowers.

Grenna has adopted Linnet as her own, of course, and not only because Gray wished it. We live together—not as man and wife, because they do not have that concept here and I will not introduce it to them. But I have taught her what *love* is and she treasures the word.

And I have sown well. In a few months Grenna will bear our child and I will *not* be forced into a second betrayal, so do not seek to bring me back.

Can you understand, sir, what I have done? Not contaminated a world but adopted one. If it is a bit changed by me—well, I have been a lot changed by it. I will continue to keep a careful record of songs and stories and customs, which I will be happy to pass on when the next anthro visit is due, in five years labtime. But I will not return to the ship; in fact, I have sent the silver tower back to you on autopilot. L'Lal'lor is my home now.

And when I die, I would be set out on pyre and pylon and be mourned by our children, because somewhere, in a Cave, I truly believe, the Gray Wanderer waits to welcome me by her side. And though I never loved her as I now do my Grenna, I know the three of us will be together as it has been prophesied we shall be.

Tape 12:

CARDS OF GRIEF

Place: Cave 27, now the center of Aerton
Time: Council time 35; labtime 2142.5 A.D.
Speaker: Grenna to Dr. M. F. Zambreno
Permission: Direct

You have come to see me about the Cards? You
have left your calling until it is almost too late. My
voice is so weak these days I can scarcely sing an
elegy without coughing, though there are those who
would tell you that singing was never my strong
point. And that is true enough. While others in the
Halls of Grief could bring in lines of mourners by
the power of their singing and others by the elo-
quence of their rhymes, such was not my way. But
many, many have come to watch me draw grief pictures on paper and board. Even now, when my
hand, which had once been called an old hand on a
young arm, is ancient beyond its years, I can still
call mourners with the power in my fingertips. Oh,
I often try to sing as I draw, in that strange high
fluting voice that one critic likened to a "slightly
demented turtle dove." But I have always known
it is the pictures, not the singing, that brings mourners to my table.

That was how Gray found me, you know, singing
in my high warble and drawing at a minor Minor
Hall for one of my dying great-great-aunts, a sister
to my mother's mother. In those days our mother
lines were quite defined.

We were a family of swineherds and had always
been so. I found it easier to talk to pigs than people;

their remarks were more direct, more truthful, more
kind. And I had never played at any Hall games with
other children, having neither brothers nor sisters,
only pigs. Once I had made up a threnody of sow-
lines. I think I could still recall it if I tried.

No matter. The irony is that I can remember the
look of my favorite sow's face, but the great-great-
aunt I mourned for, her face is lost to me forever,
though of course I know her lines: Grendi of Gren-
dinna of Grenesta and so forth.

The Gray Wanderer (she was still called that by
backwater folk like us, though all the city called her
Gray) had been on a late pilgrimage. She often went
back to country Halls. "Touching true grief," she
liked to call it, though I wonder how *true* that grief
really was. We tried to ape the court at L'Lal'dome,
and we copied their way of singing from the voice
boxes the sky-farers brought. Many of my first
drawings were tracings of their tracings. How could
I, a pigkeeper, know otherwise?

But she saw me at a Hall so minor, both pillars
and capitols were barren of carvings. There was
only an ill-conceived painting of a weeping woman
decorating one wall. Its only value was age. Paint
flaked off it like pallid scabs and no one had time
or talent to paint it anew. What it needed was not
retouching but redrawing. The arms of the woman
were stiff, the pose awkward; I knew it even then,
though I had not the words to say it.

"The girl, let me take her," the Gray Wanderer
said.

Though it was clear I had been Royal sown, being
tall and golden-eyed, I was awkward and my mother
and her sisters did not want to let me go. It was not
love that bound us but greed. I worked hard, harder

than anyone else, because I preferred it to being in their company. The pigs would suffer from my leaving. Besides, in the recent year since I had been allowed into the Hall, I had become quite a success as a griever in our small town. My mother and her sisters could not see beyond our sties to the outside world.

But the Gray Wanderer pointed out, rightfully, that they had no means to educate me beyond this Minor Hall. "Let her come with me and learn," the Gray Wanderer said, "and I will give you silks besides, to find another pigkeeper." She did not offer them touches, for she could read into their greedy, grit-filled souls.

They hesitated.

"She will bring mourners to Halls over the land to know the names of your lines, to remember you." She waved the rainbow-colored silks before their faces.

I will never know which argument decided them, but they gave me into her hands.

"You will not see her again," the Gray Wanderer told them, "except from afar. But her name will still be your name. And I promise you that she will not forget her lines."

And so it was.

And the Cards?

No, do not rush me. I will get to the Cards. But this must all come first so that you will understand.

I was sixteen summers then. Not as young as the Wanderer herself had been when she had been chosen, but young enough. Yet I left home without a backward glance, my hand on her robe. I did not even paint my tears for the leaving, it was such a small grief. I left them pawing the silks, greedier than their own swine, who sensed my leaving and mourned the only way they could, by refusing a meal. Later, I heard, my mother and one of her sisters came to L'Lal'dome and asked for more silks or at least, they said, a Lumin nut.

They were given a single silk with the embroidery of a great red lizard beast sewn on it—along with a beating.

"If you come again," the warning had been set, "she will have more names to add to the lines of grief. And they will be your own."

Well, no one likes to be called to the Cave before her time. They knew the threat for real. They did not set foot in the city again.

So I became, in effect, the Gray Wanderer's child. I would have taken her family name had she let me. But she had made a vow that I would retain my own, and she set great store by all her promises. So I kept my name, Grenna. But in all else I was hers.

I learned as much as she could teach—and more. For even when she did not teach, I learned from her by watching and listening and—as I learned later—by *loving*. It is a fine word of yours. There are, it seems, some good things that you can bring.

But Gray was already old and so all of our time added together was still short, five of our years. Excuse my tears. Crying, she used to say, is for art's sake. But of course I am not a griever now. Those who come after will grieve me.

So I come now to the part you wish to hear: about the Cards. But first I must touch upon *her* death, for it was that which inspired the Cards of Grief. It was many, many years ago, but it is still a memory clear in my mind. That is because I have never set it down. To hold in the mouth is to remember. My voice makes the telling true.

Here, let me paint it for you and tell the pictures aloud. You come from the sky and your memories are false. My paints are over there, in the round wooden box on the stand. Yes, that is the one, with the pictures of tears that look like flowers on the top. A'ron carved it for me after a story he knew from old Earth. I treasure it. Bring it to me.

First I will sketch the cave as it was, just one of the many rock outcroppings in the lower hills. You would be hard put to believe this is the same place. We have had many years to change it.

Gray and I were three days finding it, though it was the walk of one day. She knew where it was, but she had a palsy, a halting gait, that made walking slow. We camped at night under a roomom tree and watched the stars together. She told me their names, strange names they were, in your language. She knew many stories about them. Does that surprise you? It should not. The Gray Wanderer walked among you and listened. She remembered everything she ever heard you say, though she did not ape your ways.

I see.

Just as in your language you say "I *see*," meaning that you understand, we say "I *hear*." A'ron showed me that. And of course Gray's hearing was better than anyone's.

This then is the cave. The entrance was hidden behind a tight lacing of wandering thornfire. I was hours undoing it. Gray would not let me cut apart the vines.

She had discovered the cave when she had first come to be the Queen's Own Griever. Often, she told me, in that first year after her Master's death, she ran off to the hills to think. She was terribly homesick and something had angered her. Oh, I see by your face that this part of her story is known. Well, anger and homesickness were often her companions. Not mine. I had not been happy until I left my home. I would have been sick only at the thought of returning there. If I regretted anything, it was leaving my poor pigs to the mercy of my kin.

In the cave was a bed—a cot, really—constructed of roomom wood with a weaving of stripped vines strung from side to side. The thought of her dethorning those vines, strands and strands of them, here alone was enough to make me want to weep. I packed a new mattress for each of us once a week with sweet-smelling windstrife, grasses, and the musky roomom leaves. I set candles at the head and foot of the beds. There was a natural chimney near them and the smoke from the candles was drawn up it and out in a thin thread. Once I fancied it was Gray's essence slowly unwinding from her, unwinding and threading its way out of the cave. Here, I'll draw it like that. Do you see?

And then A'ron came and of course everything was changed. He and B'oremos brought the news that the Queen was dead, which made Gray both stronger and weaker. But little Linnet and her laughter filled the cave and for a time seemed to heal Gray. She breathed more easily, as if a shadow were gone from her.

If she knew that she was still dying, she did not dwell on it. If there was pain, it could only be guessed at. For the child's sake she was never sad. She was like a gourd with a new candle inside. For a while all you see is the light; you do not notice, until it is too late, that the gourd has rotted from the inside out.

She was feverish with stories and songs for the child. And she set me the same task, retelling all I remembered of the history of grieving. She wanted to set it in my memory and Linnet's for good. Since I had been with her five years, I had many, many hours of recounting to do. We spoke back and forth, an antiphony that Linnet loved. She would sway as we spoke, her little head leaning first towards me, then toward Gray.

When we had gotten to the end of all the tales, Gray added a new story, one whose parts I had only heard from others. And she spoke it to me alone. I remember it as if she just told it this morning. It was her own tale.

She did not put A'ron in it by name, nor did she mention Linnet. Perhaps that is because she had been sworn to another truth by the old Queen, whose death sealed her in that lie.

But that day, when the telling was done, when Linnet and A'ron were off picking wildflowers, Gray bade me bring her the Cup of Sleep, putting her hand out to me—thus. I can scarcely draw her fingers as thin and gnarled as they were then. It makes me ache to see them again, but that is not what stops me. Drawing them requires a delicacy that, alas, my old hands have forgot. But as thin and pale and hollowed out as she was, her hair was still that vigorous electric dark it had always been. I plaited it as she instructed, with red trillis for life and blue-black mourning berries for death. I twined green boughs around the bed for her passage in between.

Then she smiled at me and comforted me when she saw I would weep—I, who rarely wept for anything in my life.

I stood there with the Cup in my hand. Does the figure look strange to you? A bit cramped? Well, it should. My back and neck hurt from the tension of wanting to give her the Cup to ease her pain, and yet not wanting to because though her pain would be over, Linnet and A'ron and I would have pain that would go on and on and on. Of course in the end I gave her the Cup and left as she bid, before she drank, before I could stop her from drinking.

I stood outside the cave and think I drew the first real breath of air since giving her the Cup, and just then A'ron and Linnet came back from their walk. The child was carrying a straggly bouquet of limp moons'cap and trillis and those little yellow wildflowers whose center are shaped like eyes, I forget their names.

Wood-cheese or Wood's eye.

You have studied our world well. A'ron was right to admire you. Well, I moved quickly down the path to meet them and made up a story to keep them from the cave. As we walked—with the child running before us, chirruping and leading the way—I had to smile. A'ron caught my hand as we walked. We often just touched that way. If it meant payment, I did not reckon for what. And something suddenly broke apart deep within me. I thought it was the grief, but A'ron looked at me.

"You are laughing, Grenna," he said. "Listen, Linnet, your mama can laugh." But she was already too far along the path to hear or care. He spun me toward him and touched my face with his fingers.

But my eyes were filled with tears and when he saw that, he guessed.

"Gray?" he asked.

I nodded.

And he began to cry, soundlessly at first, and then with great heaving sobs. I had never heard the like. I held him and when he stopped making the noise, I drew his face down to mine and kissed away his tears.

That was how Linnet found us, crying and kissing. And she held her hands up to us so that she might be picked up and touched, too. And we both kissed her and she put the flowers on our heads and said, "Now you both belong to me and to each other."

Ah, Dot'der'tsee, you have tears in your eyes, too. Do you cry for the death of the Gray Wanderer?

I am not sure, Grenna. I cry about some loss, anyway.

But nothing can be lost, Dot'der'tsee, if you hold it in your mouth and ear. If it is remembered, it is not lost.

Then I do not know why I am crying. Please, continue the story.

We put Linnet down and she skipped up the path and into the cave before I could stop her. When she cried out, we ran in.

Gray was lying as I had left her, her face composed, her hands laced together. It surprised me to see her look so young and beautiful.

A'ron and I brought her husk out and put it up on the pylons. Gray and I had built them months before, though in truth she had only watched, her hand pressed against her side, while I had done the work.

I sat a whole day, still as a stone, not speaking to A'ron, though often I cuddled Linnet on my lap. I sat until the first birds came and settled on Gray's husk and one, a black bird with wild white eyes, took the first bite.

Then I fled down the mountainside, holding Linnet in my arms, and we were both sick several times, though I had sat a pyrewatch before and had never blanched. It is odd how one can be sick with nothing in the stomach but bile.

I left Linnet with A'ron and went down the mountainside to the city, directly to the King's Apartments, and knelt and said, "The Gray Wanderer is gone."

"You will make them remember her?" he asked. It was a proper response, but I had wanted something more from him. I knew how he had treasured her.

"Your Majesty," I said, giving him back ice for ice, "I will."

"May your lines of grieving be long," he said.

I turned and left. He knew that I had left out the last line of the ritual. I would not give him the satisfaction of my words. He would not hear "May your time of dying be short" from me. I did not care then if his were short or long. The one I cared about had already had too many betrayals, too long a time of dying, too short a time of living.

I went back to the cave, remembering her words. I pinched my cheeks for color and sat down with A'ron's gi'tarr to compose a small dirge, a threnody, a lament. I had become fond of the sweetness of the strings and he had given me the gi'tarr for my own.

But nothing came. Even Gray's own words were too soft for my feelings.

I stared at my reflection in the small mirror I had put up for Linnet, who had a child's passion for such things. Real tears marked a passage down my cheeks. I could have painted over them with tear lines in any color I wanted, but I could not just paint my face and let her go.

I spoke to her under my breath: "Forgive me, Gray. Forgive my excess of sorrow." She would have shuddered at the ocean of tears. But though I was no girl of her lines, I was her true apprentice. She was dearer to me than a line mother and I had to do something more to honor her. She would have long, long lines of mourners to remember her. I would give her immortality for sure.

So all that next night, in the Royal Hall of Grief, with mourners passing in and out, speaking their ritual parts with as much or as little sincerity as they could manage, I began to devise the Cards. A'ron kept Linnet away, because if they had been there to mourn with me, I could not have borne it.

I was silent while I worked and it may be that it was my silence that first called the mourners in, for if I had any reputation at all as a young griever, it was not for silence. *Sharp-tongued* was one of the kinder things that was said of me. But if it was the silence that drew them in, it was the Cards of Grief that brought them back.

It took a week of sleepless days and nights before I was done with the painting. And then I returned to the cave, where I slept for a solid week, hardly knowing who I was or what I was or where it was I was sleeping. I did not even know that while I slept, A'ron—to contain his own grief—was building a house around me, a house as unlike a cave as it could be, filled with light and sky. When at last I really woke to my surroundings, my hands were so stained with paint that it was months before they were clean again. A'ron said that each time he had tried to clean my fingers, I had fought him with a fury that could not be restrained. I would not have believed him except he showed me his eye, which I had blacked, and I kissed it many times in an effort to beg forgiveness, which he laughed away. The clothes I had worn for that week I burned. I never recovered my memory of that seven days. I had only A'ron's word for what happened, but I believed him. He never lied.

I brought Gray a line of grievers as has never been seen before or since—long, solemn rows: young and old, men as well as women, children who had never once seen her grieve. Even the sky-farers came, borne in by curiosity I am sure, but staying to weep with the rest. You are, it seems, a people of Occasional Tears. And each time the Cards are seen, another griever is added to her lines. Oh, the Gray Wanderer is an immortal for sure.

I was there. I was one of those sky-farers who wept her down.

Were you? I do not remember you.

I am hard not to remember. You must not have seen me.

You are correct; it is impolite for me to say that to you. But I am glad that you were there.

And what of the Cards?

The Cards? I have not forgotten. Here, put the paints away. That little painting? It is nothing, just a quick sketch.

May I keep it?

Certainly. And each time you look at it, you will remember Gray.

I would have liked to have known her more.

You would have liked her? I see you know our rituals. So I will answer you in kind. She would have grown by your friendship. And *that* is quite true. Though she eschewed the ways of your people, she did not forget to grow in her art by understanding. And of course she *loved* A'ron before he became one of the People, one of us.

Yes.

And now the Cards. You see, I have not forgotten. *Now* is the time to show you.

Is this how you want them?

Set them here.

The first pack was an eleven, not the more ornate thirteen plus thirteen that gamesters use. I drew the Cards on a heavy paper that I made of soaked and pressed reeds. I drew lightly so that only I could really discern the outline. Then I colored them in with the paints and chalks I used for my grief masks. That is why the colors are so basic, not the wider palette of art, but the monochromatic range of the body's grief paints. The red? That color has been so remarked upon. Here is the truth of it. It was not paint at all. It was my own blood. I drew it from the soft inside of my left elbow, the turning closest to the heart. You can still see the scar. It is no more than a raised pinprick now. A'ron said that was why I slept so long after. Not from exhaustion or from grief. I had a disease of the blood for which he had begged medicines from your ship. When he was given none by your people . . .

He knew we could not. It is against all our vows.

He held me through my fever, even when I raged
and beat on him with my fists. Even when Linnet
cried, he held me. There is nothing to show of that
fever but the scar. I do not remember. . . .

The Cards?

To this day the original thirteen is called the
Prime Pack. Does that confuse you? You are counting on your fingers. There were eleven done at the
Hall of Grief and then, after my week of fever and
sleep, I rose and painted two more. The Prime Pack
is kept on velvet in the Council Museum, under
glass. They are arranged at each month's turning in
a new order, as if the order matters now.

That first pack spoke directly to my need. There
was no arcane symbology. The Seven Grievers were
one card for each of the seven great families. The
Cave That Is Fed By No Light, the darkest card, is
of course the death card. For as we come from the
womb cave, so we go to that other cave in the end,
and, of course, my beloved Gray came to her end
in a real cave. The picture on the card is an exact
rendering of her last resting, the bed in the cave's
center, twined with trillis and mourning berry, her
bed.

The Queen of Shadows is the major card, for
Gray was always loyal to her Queen. And the Singer
of Dirges is the minor card. The moving card, the
card that can go with ease from high place to low,
was the card I called after her, my Master, the Gray
Wanderer. Its face is her face and the dark hair
under the gray cloak is twined with flowers. But it
is the Wanderer as she was young, not crabbed with
age and pain; when her face was unlined and she
had a sky prince for a lover.

Seven Grievers. The Cave. The Queen. The

Singer. The Gray Wanderer. Eleven cards in all.
And, after my sleep, I added two: The Man Without
Tears and the Cup of Sleep.

I sometimes think it was only a sentimental gesture. Gray often warned me about confusing sen-
timent with sentimentality. I wonder what she
would have thought of it. But I meant it for her; I
meant it as all true grievers mean the poems and
scriptings and songs and pictures we make. Those
are the old, slow ways, but for all that they are old
and slow, they are about birth and death and the
small passage we travel between.

I did not have to explain the Cards to the many
lines of mourners who came to honor Gray. Not the
way I have to explain them today. Over and over,
to those like you who come from the sky; to my own
people who now ape grief with comic songs and
dances and who have turned even the Cards of Grief
into a game.

But I will do it one more time. One final time. I
will tell the Prime Pack. Forgive me if the telling is
one whose parts you have heard before. This time
I will tell it with infinite care, for there are times
that I—even I—have told them as a rota, a list,
without meaning. This time I will unwind the thread
of honest grief. For the Gray Wanderer. For myself.
For A'ron and Linnet and the rest. The story, the
story must be told till the end.

I will lay out the Cards, one by one by one. Listen
well. Do not rely on your boxes, sky woman. Use
your eyes. Use your ears. Memory is the daughter
of the eye and ear.

*I will listen and see, Grenna. I will turn off the
box and hold the memory in my ears and in my
mouth.*

Good, Dot'der'tsee. That is how it should be.

Here are the Seven Grievers.

One is for Lands as I am from Lands, for all those who work the soil. We were here before all the rest and we will remain when all the rest are forgotten. Lands wears the brown tunic and trews of my family and rides a white sow.

Two is for Moon, for those who count the season's turning, seers and priestess who speak the prophesies and carry rood and orb.

Three is for Arcs and Bow, who hunt the forests and fields.

Four is for Waters and all who plow there.

Five is for Rocks, who scrape the mountain's face and craft gems from the stone.

Six is for Stars, who script our poems, whose memories are short, who study and forget.

Seven, the Queen's Own, the tall Royals. They came from the sea, twinned, to rule us.

Seven Grievers who were touched by my Master's words.

And from those Seven, now come these. Queen of Shadows to rule them. Singer of Dirges to betray them. The Cup of Sleep to change them. The Man Without Tears to watch them change. The Gray Wanderer, who speaks of them all till she enters the Cave of No Light.

That was how I told them then, in a singsong voice dripping with tears. That first thirteen were known as the Cards of Dark, for all the faces on the original pack were dark, since I drew them in my grief. The thirteen cards added later by the gamesters were called Cards of Light, and all the figures grin, their whitened faces set in a rictus, a parody of all we hold sacred.

Here, you can see the difference even in this pack. In my drawing of the Man Without Tears, he wears a landing suit and holds his hands outstretched by his side, the light streaming through a teardrop in each palm. But his face cannot be seen, obscured as it is by the bubble of his headgear. Yet in the gamesters' thirteen, he wears a different uniform, in blue, with stars and bars on the shoulders. He has a beard. And though his hands are still outstretched, with the light reflecting through the palm, his face is drawn as plain as any griever's and he smiles. It is a painful, sad grimace.

You can see the difference also in the Queen of Shadows. In my pack, she is dressed in red and black and her picture is a dark portrait of the Queen who had been on the throne when Gray was master of them all. But the packs today are no-faced and every-faced, the features as bland as the mash one feeds a child. There is no meaning there. *My* Queen wore a real face, narrow, feral, devious, hungry, sad. But the Card looked back to an even older tale. You know it? The Queen mourning her dead chief consort went into the Cave at the Center of the World. She wore a red dress and a black cloak and carried a bag of her most precious jewels to buy back his release from Death. In those days Death was thought to live in a great stone palace in the world's center surrounded by circles of unmourned folk who had to grieve for themselves. Death was not satisfied with a Royal touch, seeing that, in the end, Death could touch and be touched by any and by all.

The Queen followed the winding, twisting cave for miles, learning to see in the dark land with a night sight as keen as any Common Griever. Many long nights passed and at last she stopped by a pool and knelt down to drink. She saw, first, the dartings of phosphorescent fish, as numerous as stars. Then she saw, staring up from the pool, her own reflection with its shining night eyes, big and luminous. She did not recognize herself, so changed was she by her journey; but thought it a Queen from the night sky, fallen from the stars. She so desired the image that she stayed by the poolside, weeping her precious gems into it, begging the jewel-eyed woman to come to her.

After thirteen days of weeping, her grief for her consort was forgot and her gems were all gone. She returned home empty-handed, babbling of the Queen who fell from the sky. Her eyes remained wide and dark-seeing, a visionary and a seeress who spoke in riddles and read signs in the stars and was never again quite sane. She was called the Queen of Shadows.

You do not understand the other Cards in the deck? The Singer of Dirges is, of course, named after B'oremos when he was on his mission year. He brought my Master her fame but betrayed her three times. That is why on the Card he wears three faces. And so the Singer Card within the deck helps the other Cards move in three ways through the pattern, up or down, side to side, or on a diagonal through time.

And the Cup? It is the changer. If it precedes a Card, it changes the Card and its pattern. If it follows a Card, it does no harm. The only Card it cannot change is the Cave.

When I first told the rota, I only told it bare of all this. "One is for Lands . . ." I said. But over the years I have considered the rest and that is what I tell you now.

So now I know the Cards as well as you do, but still I do not know why you made them.

To help me grieve, sky-farer. To remember Gray.

I think there is more.

What more can there be? The Cards are my grief. Oh, now they are used by all the People as a game, telling the future, retelling the past. They make common what was singular. They have taken what was mine and made it. . . .

Their own. Perhaps that is because we are each a Card in the Cards of Grief. We feel your Cards, even when we know it not, here, here in the heart. You are yourself like the Singer, helping others move within the pattern, pointing the way.

Then you and yours, sky woman, are what? Like Cups of Sleep you have dealt death to our old ways. You observe us, change us, go away. Gray knew this but was powerless to stop it. So am I. So I point the way for Linnet and the children with her on the Council; I point and they lead the way? Is that what you mean?

Then I will tell you a secret, Dot'der'tsee, a secret I have shared with no one, not even my A'ron. Would you know it?

I would if you would tell it to me.

I tell it to you because A'ron, before he died, confessed to me that his people would come down one more time and, when they saw what was happening, would go away and never return. That is why I show it to you now.

The bottom of the box that A'ron carved is a false bottom. And if you slide it, thus, there are two last Cards I have never shown, for they are not Cards of Grief at all. I made them the year after Gray's death. One Card is called the Laughing Man, the other the Child of Earth and Sky.

They are—quite beautiful. And I would know them both, anywhere. The man, with the child in each arm, the blond hair and that lopsided grin. It is Aaron.

Those are our children, a boy and a girl, a wonder rarely seen in our world. *Twins.* Is it any wonder that A'ron is laughing?

No wonder.

And the Child of Earth and Sky—

You do not have to tell me. A year older, but still the same. She is little Linnet, my godchild.

She rules now, with a Council of children, though they are no longer young, with B'oremos to advise them. So many changes. Gray warned us of them. And the prophesies, too, warned that if we forsake grief, our world will die. But A'ron promised me it did not have to be so. I believed him. He was a man who did not lie.

No, he did not lie.

Your eyes fill up again, Dot'der'tsee. Perhaps you are trying to grieve for A'ron. I would help you if I could, but my tears dried up with his death. And my laughter. There is only a hard bitter core, like a Lumin kernel, inside. A'ron did not lie, ever. But he did not tell me the truth about loving, either. Never did he say that to love makes dying difficult.

Perhaps he wanted to learn your way, not teach his own. He had long carried a piece of angry wisdom within him. It said, "It is a fearful thing to love what death can touch." When he came here, when he loved you, I think he believed that he had found a place that death could not really touch. He loved you for it.

But I do not understand. We die.

You die. You grieve. But you are not really touched by death. At least that is what Aaron wanted to believe. He was always such a romantic boy.

He loved you, Dot'der'tsee. We called our girl Mairi for you.

I know. We have—ways of knowing.

Then you knew of A'ron's dying?

Yes.

But you did not come down to grieve?

It was not the time.

He knew that, though I think he hoped. . . .

He was old. And I—I would not have been changed by time. It would not have been—right— for me to come then. It would have been against our vows.

He knew that. He left you a message.

May I see it?

You must listen. He did not write it down. The message is this: Linnet is the bridge, the child of earth and sky. She speaks two languages, she knows two times, she sings all songs. Trust her. She remembers you, Dot'der'tsee; she does not forget.

So Linnet is the final Card, hidden until now? A Card of Joy. Even though he knew it not, she is the Card up Aaron's sleeve. No wonder he laughs in your picture. Oh, Aaron Spenser, you died young, as I remember you. I am far older than you would believe.

I am glad that I showed the Cards to you.

Not so glad as I. I would embrace you, Grenna.
I would be embraced.

So much telling. My mouth is dry. Hand me that
Cup, the one on the table.
The black one? It is a lovely thing.
Yes, isn't it. The engravings are quite old. It belonged to Gray's family. B'oremos knew of it, don't
ask me how, and gave it to me when the twins were
born. We named the boy after him and he was so
pleased he almost laughed. I need to moisten my
tongue. There, that is good.
*What does the writing mean? It is in a script I
do not know.*
It means "Here is the Cup. Take it willingly. May
your time of dying be short."
Do not look so startled. I know what I do. And
now you know, too. But Dot'der'tsee, you have
studied our culture so many years. Have you not
learned it well? There is no penalty here for giving
a peaceful death. I am ready and I have confessed.
My words are in your box. Oh, I know you turned
it off, but I know also that there is a box here in this
cave. A'ron told me, which is why I chose to die
here. I would have spoken all this to the walls if you
had not arrived.

My children know what it is I do and they are
satisfied that I die in peace. Who do you think got
the Lumin for me? My dying will be short.

But you can do something for me, something that
will not violate your vows. When you grieve for
A'ron, grieve for me as well. Grieve for all of us in
this quiet, changing land. You owe us that immortality at least.

Good, I see tears again in your eyes. And these are spilling down, a refreshing rain of them.

Will you stay with me and hold my hand and wipe the tears for A'ron that are pooling in my eyes? I thank you for them, Dot'der'tsee. I understand now that I needed to grieve with someone; I could not grieve for him alone. He belonged to both of us—you and me, your world and mine.

Now I feel the long sleep coming on me. The time of my dying will be short. I hope that my lines of mourning will be very long, for I would stay with my beloved Gray Wanderer and the Laughing Man in the Cave that is beyond all of your stars.

TIME LINE

Planet	Lab	History
Queen's Time 1, Thirteenth Matriarchy	2130 A.D.	Discovery of Henderson's IV; first preset recorders in place; Queen is twenty years old.
Queen's Time 10, Thirteenth Matriarchy	2131 A.D.	Lina–Lania/the Gray Wanderer born.
Queen's Time 23, Thirteenth Matriarchy	2132.5 A.D.	Linni enters first Hall of Grief; writes first Gray Wanderer poems; found by B'oremos.
Queen's time 23–24, Thirteenth Matriarchy	2132.5+ A.D.	Gray enter's Queen's service, has her year of training; the Queen is thirty-five. *THE SEVEN GRIEVERS I, II, III*
Queen's Time 25, Thirteenth Matriarchy	2132.5+ A.D.	Gray becomes the Queen's Own Griever.
Queen's Time 26, Thirteenth Matriarchy	2132.8 A.D.	Planetfall . . . first landing of sky-farers; the "death" of Dr. Z; Linni/Gray and Aaror Spenser fall in love. She is twenty, he is twenty-two.
Queen's Time 26, Thirteenth Matriarchy	2132.9 A.D.	Aaron is Court Martialed; Gray gives birth; the child Linnet is brought to the lab. *THE MAN WITHOUT TEARS*
Queen's Time 27–76, Thirteenth Matriarchy	2132.9–2137 A.D.	Aaron's five-year exile aboard space lab, where he raises the child; on the planet Gray turns only to her art, where she is the Master Griever for fifty years.
Queen's Time 70, Thirteenth Matriarchy	2137 A.D.	Gray discovers the pigkeeper's daughter, Grenna, who becomes her apprentice, all but adopts her. Gray is sixty, Grenna sixteen.
Queen's Time 76, Thirteenth Matriarchy	2137.5 A.D.	Aaron returns. He is twenty-seven, child is five, Gray is sixty-five, Grenna twenty-one. Queen is ninety-six, looks young. Aa'on confronts Queen with B'oremos listening in. Queen dies. B'oremos is King. *QUEEN OF SHADOWS*
King's Time 1, First Patriarchy	2137.5+ A.D.	Aaron finds Gray, meets Grenna, Gray dies. *THE SINGER OF DIRGES, PRINCE OF TRAITORS, BETRAYALS, THE CHILD OF EARTH AND SKY IN THE HALL OF GRIEF TRANSMISSION TO COMMAND*
Council Time 35	2142.5 A.D.	Linnet and others rule with guidance of B'oremos; death of Grenna, confessing to Dr. Z, who has returned for final anthro visit. *CARDS OF GRIEF*